BATTLEMAGE REDUX

BATTLEMAGE REDUX

GO ASK YOUR MOTHER™ BOOK 3

THEOPHILUS MONROE

MICHAEL ANDERLE

DON'T MISS OUR NEW RELEASES

Join the LMBPN email list to be notified of new releases and special promotions (which happen often) by following this link:

http://lmbpn.com/email/

Copyright © 2023 LMBPN Publishing
Cover by Fantasy Book Design
Cover copyright © LMBPN Publishing
A Michael Anderle Production

LMBPN Publishing
PMB 196, 2540 South Maryland Pkwy
Las Vegas, NV 89109

Version 1.00, April 2023
ebook ISBN: 979-8-88541-363-3
Print ISBN: 979-8-88878-348-1

THE BATTLEMAGE REDUX TEAM

Thanks to our JIT Readers

Christopher Gilliard
Diane L. Smith
Jackey Hankard-Brodie
Jeff Goode
Veronica Stephan-Miller
Paul Westman
Jan Hunnicutt

Editor
The Skyhunter Editing Team

CHAPTER ONE

Nigel and I faced off in an old training room in the hospital-turned-alliance headquarters in St. Louis. The air was thick with the smell of disinfectant.

It was a new spell I'd been practicing. I'd seen him use it when we fought Hana's undead mages. He taught me how to do it.

I held my wand in two hands, and a beam of arcane energy flowed from the tip.

Nigel held up his wand and did the same. "Low energy, remember. Our strikes should only give us a little shock."

I gave a slight nod and a mischievous smirk. I reached out to one of the tables to retrieve my Darth Vader helmet. I put it on over my head. It was a bit tight, but it worked. I'd been waiting for this moment ever since I saw Nigel cast the spell from his wand in the battle.

I waved my wand-slash-arcane saber in front of my face. I dropped my voice as low as I could, which was unnecessary because my helmet had a voice filter that made me sound just like James Earl Jones. "The circle is now complete... Now *I am the master!*"

Nigel rolled his eyes. "Wanker."

I widened my stance and prepared to strike. Nigel's button-up shirt was stuck to his skin with sweat, and his slender black tie dangled from his neck. It was better than the three-piece suit he wore all the time when I first met him. And he called *me* the wanker? All right. I was a grown-ass man in his forties doing Darth Vader cosplay. Come on, though. What man wouldn't do that if he could make an arcane saber like mine?

I lunged at Nigel and swung my saber at him. He easily blocked the attack, single-handedly. His other hand was placed confidently on his waist.

I pivoted my hips and struck again, this time from the opposite side. Once again, he effortlessly blocked my sword with his own.

"What was that nonsense about the circle? Who did you say the master was now?"

I huffed. "Nigel, I am your daddy!"

Nigel snorted. His saber blocked two of my swings, and I felt the sharp sting as it caught me around the back of my leg. The energy struck me like an electric shock. My leg went temporarily numb.

"Is that so, mate? Looks like you got it backward."

I hopped on one leg, trying to jab Nigel with my saber. He laughed and gracefully stepped aside each time as he whisked away my saber with his own.

Nigel casually struck my other leg, and I fell to my knees.

"You won't stop me that easily!"

Nigel laughed. "I am Arthur, King of the Britons."

"What are you talking about?"

Nigel tapped me with his saber on one arm. My arm went limp. I dropped my wand and picked it up again with my opposite hand. "'Tis but a scratch, right, mate? Just a flesh wound?"

I grunted. "Dare you mock a Sith Lord?"

Nagel laughed. "You're a lot less Darth Vader right now and a lot more of Monty Python's Black Knight. Give it a minute and your feeling will return. You need to learn how to properly handle your weapon. You can't swing your saber around like some kind of loony and expect to prevail against a trained swordsman."

"You told me to practice. Look at my saber. It's pretty badass, right?"

"The sharpest katana in the hand of a samurai is a powerful tool. In the hand of a fool, it is dangerous."

"Are you saying I'm a fool?"

"Of course not. You have a gift. Wisdom inherited from your grandfather. Still, you do a great job of covering it up with nonsense."

Feeling returned to my arms and legs, and I removed my Darth Vader helmet. "So I practiced. I can draw my arcane saber from my core. It's pure and strong."

"Still, you must learn how to wield it. It's an effective weapon for a battlemage. Much better in close combat than arcane missiles or even cherry bombs. You shouldn't try to use it, though, unless you are confident that you can best your opponent."

"I held my own with that chainsaw before. When Hana attacked us at the store."

"You were fighting zombies, Thomas. Animated corpses of Entente mages that Hana killed just hours before. They were muscle, a tool she used to try and break through your gates and distract you. They were hardly skilled fighters."

I took a deep breath. "I'm sorry, man. You know how I am. When I'm insecure about something, I cover it up with sarcasm and humor."

"Why are you insecure?" Nigel asked. "There's no shame in acknowledging that you still have much to learn. There is *great* shame in pretending you're a master when you're a novice. Recognizing your deficiencies is necessary if you want to improve."

I cleared my throat. "Growth areas."

Nigel raised an eyebrow. "What?"

"I'm taking a course on management and leadership online. Working on my management degree. I figured it would help. Both with the tool rental store and for leading the alliance. They call our weaknesses 'growth areas,' not 'deficiencies.' It's all about positive self-speak and whatnot."

"It doesn't matter what you call your weaknesses—"

I raised my index finger. "Growth areas!"

Nigel cleared his throat. "That sounds like skin cancer. Might want to get your moles checked, mate."

"It's called leadership!"

"Positive self-talk isn't helpful if it gets you killed. You have weaknesses, Thomas. So do I. So does everyone."

"In my class, they said we shouldn't use words that motivate from a place of fear. We should focus on a positive vision instead. A place of hope."

"We're looking at a war with the new Axis, Thomas. In business, I suppose hope is better than fear. In a battle, you bloody better have a good dose of healthy fear. You need not honor your enemy, but you should respect their skill. Fear can be a powerful motivator if you channel it correctly."

I scratched the back of my head. "It can also be paralyzing."

"If you cower in the face of fear, you bet your blimey arse it can be."

I snorted. "I know what you're saying. I get it, all right? I need to learn how to fight with a saber."

Nigel pocketed his wand and placed his hand on my shoulder. "When I was just a lad, I accidentally kicked a football over my neighbor's fence. I was only nine or ten. About the age of your oldest. When I climbed the fence to get it, a large Doberman took off out of his doghouse after me, growling and snarling. Now, I've never been much of a jumper or a climber, but I leaped over the top of that fence and pulled myself to safety in a half-second.

If not for fear, I could have tried to do that a hundred times and failed every time. With a healthy fear, a fear that recognized the fact that a big snarling Doberman could tear me to pieces, I transcended my limits."

"Adrenaline, most likely."

Nigel nodded. "Certainly. But after that, I believed I could do it. Once I did it, it didn't matter much that it was fear that first pushed me to the next level. What mattered is I knew I could do it. After that, I scaled fences with an ease I never had before."

I cleared my throat. "I get it. Fear is good. I need to practice more."

Nigel shook his head. "Sometimes fear challenges us to rise to the occasion. It can happen in a split second, like when that dog came after me, or it can happen over time. This is an occasion when a good fear of Hana and the Axis mages should inspire you to excel beyond what you ever thought possible before. That's not being negative. It's using everything and anything to push yourself to be better. It's a positive thing."

I put Wand in my back pocket and leaned against the wall. "I am afraid to die."

"Most people are."

I pinched my chin. "You know what I fear more than death?"

"Tell me, Thomas."

"I fear failing to protect my family. I fear something happening to them because of me. Because the enemy knew they could use them against me. Because I wasn't good enough or strong enough to keep them safe."

"So you have a healthy long-term fear. There's nothing stronger than that. What do you say we put that split-second fear to the test?"

"What do you mean?" I asked.

Nigel retrieved his wand and formed his glowing blue arcane saber at the end. "A little stronger this time. Enough to knock you out cold and leave you with one hell of a headache. I've already taught you the basic blocks. Can you block me?"

I gulped. I pulled Wand from my back pocket and formed my saber. "I don't know. I can try."

"Not a good enough answer, Thomas. You better be able to, because I will not lower the power. You either block me or you pay for it."

Nigel came at me with a fury. I raised my wand-saber and blocked his first strike. He pivoted his hips and swung at my legs. I jumped over his saber. He made a full circle with his saber in one arm and brought it down at me from above. My arm reacted and I stopped his saber just before it struck me over the top of my head.

He laughed. "I knew you could do it. Now, let's go over some basic strikes. It's one thing to block your enemy. Eventually, no matter how good you are, they'll get lucky. Unless you know how to counterstrike."

CHAPTER TWO

I pocketed my wand and twisted my back. Forty-two isn't the best age to learn how to joust. My back was as unpredictable as any enemy I'd ever faced. I always knew when it happened. I'd feel something move in my back, a sudden but initially tolerable wave of pain, and over the next few hours, all the muscles around the spot would end up in full-on spasm mode.

I was pretty sure I got out of this particular training session with my back intact. That didn't mean I could let my guard down. When my back went out, it never happened because I was doing something strenuous. It was usually at some point afterward. I could go to the gym and do six sets of deadlifts without a problem. It was when I'd bend over later that night to pick up a sock that the pain wave would strike.

I popped a couple of ibuprofen and did my best to smear a glob of Bengay around my low back and shoulders. The mid-back was still vulnerable. I couldn't reach it, and I wasn't about to ask Nigel to rub my back with Bengay.

I grew up in the eighties and nineties, and I was raised to avoid physical contact with other dudes whenever possible. Never use a urinal directly next to another man. Always leave a "buffer" urinal in between. Also, don't ever rub anything into another man's skin. I knew it was silly. Nothing about applying muscle relaxer called someone's sexual orientation into question, and if it did, so what? I believed in acceptance and equality. Still, if you grew up when I did, old habits rooted in archaic phobias died hard.

That I'd rather risk leaving my mid-back vulnerable to seizing up than allow a man to touch my back-skin was patently ridiculous. I knew it. I was well aware that it was dumb and rooted in backward prejudices and insecurities. I also knew I couldn't help the fact that something about man-to-man contact was more likely to make my back seize up than it was to help me relax.

Nigel and I talked a lot about fear. What he didn't address was why facing my dumbest and most irrational fears was sometimes harder than confronting a life-threatening force of evil.

He could swing his saber at me with a charge that was going to knock me out, and I rose to the occasion and blocked every strike. Hana Sato could raise the corpses of mages and send them at me, and I'd cut them down with a chainsaw.

It was a different thing to face a fear, no matter how old-school and backward, that represented a wall in my mind erected in my formative years that was supposed to make me more secure in my identity. All the while, I suspected, it was because no one was ever really secure about their identity. We build false walls in our minds, trying to close in on our true selves. All the while, what we're left with is a shadow of who we are, a caricature and a facade that we use to present to others, and ourselves, because nothing is more terrifying than self-discovery. What if we find out that we aren't who we want to be? What if we aren't what other people expect us to be?

Muscle relaxers aside, that was what haunted me more than my fears. Who was I to lead an alliance of mages? Why would anyone follow me, an American mage, when the Entente mages were raised following a strict code that didn't line up with my worldview? What if my leadership philosophy was bullshit? Maybe everything I learned in class, this new-school philosophy of leading through casting a vision, creating ownership in the vision, and inspiring people to rise to the occasion was little more than sentimental drivel, meant to coddle people rather than challenge them to do better? Nigel thought fear had a place in my training, in leadership, but my teachers in my online business program didn't think it was worth anything.

That was my biggest fear. That everything I was pretending to be wasn't real. Despite my history of being headstrong and a little arrogant when I went into battle, at my core, I had my doubts. What if I was one big fat fraud? What if following me got people killed?

While I was training with Nigel, my nine-year-old son, Elijah, was training in portal magery.

When we'd set up the headquarters for the new Mage Alliance, we used an old hospital on Jefferson. Professor Pritchard, who I often referred to as Prof. Poppycock, was running the mage academy. It wasn't the residential program he ran in the Entente chambers. It was an after-school program. The mages in the alliance sent their children to secular schools for their basic education, and they came to the headquarters three nights a week. Two of those nights were with Poppycock, learning about arcane theory, the history of magery, and whatnot. Those young mages who'd specialized, like my son, spent Wednesday evenings training with their mentors.

Elijah's mentor was Evander, a young gate mage who'd played a pivotal role in saving the survivors from the Entente chambers during Hana's attack. The apple didn't fall far from the tree. Elijah wasn't a fan of classroom studies, but he loved training and working on his gate mage skills.

My two younger sons, Ezra and Elliot, five and three respectively, wouldn't likely manifest for a few more years—if they ever did. Being the first-born, Elijah had some advantages. He got to do all of this first. Kat and I weren't sure how we could manage his abilities. Gate mages can get into a lot of trouble. With a single portal, Elijah could easily reach into other people's homes, businesses, or whatever, and take whatever he wanted. He was old enough to know that stealing was wrong. He was also old enough that he had secrets of his own. Thievery was only one worry. He could also hide things he wasn't supposed to have in a portal that could stash his stuff virtually anywhere.

For the time being, thankfully, Elijah's range was limited. Unlike Hans or Evander, he couldn't create gates all over the world. He couldn't even make any large enough to accommodate his entire body. So far, all he'd done was create small portals he could reach through and use to engage in his prepubescent shenanigans. The worst he did at his age, such as stealing Twinkies from the neighbor's pantry or dumping his broccoli off his plate and into the yard, was harmless compared to the trouble he could get into if he didn't learn to wield his abilities responsibly.

Once he turned sixteen, he'd have a chance to enter an ethereal realm and claim a wand. That's when his power would magnify and intercontinental travel might become possible. What was important now was to teach control and responsibility. He who can be faithful with a little can be trusted with much.

It worked out well that I trained with Nigel whenever Elijah was in class or working with Evander. While I waited outside the room where Evander and Elijah were working, Hans approached, shuffling his feet.

"Hey, Hans! How goes it?"

"Not bad, Tom. How's your training going?"

I shrugged. "We're getting there. A lot of relatively simple lessons that apparently I'm choosing to learn the hard way."

Hans smirked. "That sounds like you."

"What is that supposed to mean?" I raised my eyebrows.

"It means you can be a stubborn bastard, sometimes. It's not necessarily a flaw. It can be. Your stubbornness probably saved my life when the American mages voted to kill me."

I rubbed my brow. "That wasn't stubbornness. It was decency."

"Exactly. They thought if they killed me, they'd seal the arcane breach. They thought that one boy's life was worth stopping the mist from spreading. Of course, they didn't know the true nature of the threat. But you were stubborn. You made my grandfather a promise. You stuck to it because you knew it was the right thing to do. I owe my life to your stubborn ass."

I chuckled. "Well, I appreciate you saying so. How is your grandmother doing?"

"She's been meeting with Mary and Jessie. They're the only three empaths so they've been getting together, singing Kumbaya, and practicing their skills."

"And it's helping Rose?"

Hans nodded. "My grandmother still has dementia. Funny, though, how much working with other empaths can help heal the mind. Things my grandmother forgets, Jessie and Mary can help her bring back to the forefront of her mind."

"That's good to hear. Face it, though, her issues were deeper than that. She thought it was 1943 back after Hana captured the two of you."

"That was as much the work of Goebbels, the Axis empath, as it was her own desire to retreat to the past in her mind. Now that Mary taught her and Jessie how to deal with the problem of those painful empath feedback loops when they connected to each other, having other empaths who understand what she's going through is really helping. She may not ever be back to a hundred percent, but she knows who I am. She doesn't mistake me for my father anymore. She knows what's at stake."

"That's good to hear. How is your room here? You're always welcome back at my place if you're uncomfortable here."

Hans shifted his eyes back and forth. "Honestly, no disrespect intended, but it's great. I have my own room. There are dozens of domestic mages here. My room is *always* clean and I can be a total slob, no problem. And there's the food. Don't get me wrong, Kat can heat up a mean frozen lasagna, but these domestic mages are like gourmet chefs."

I smirked. "Yeah, I love the cafeteria here. It doesn't look like much down there, but I'm not sure there's anything those domestic mages *can't* cook well. Want to know a secret?"

Hans tilted his head. "Sure."

"Sometimes I eat here before I go home. Especially on mac and cheese nights."

Hans chuckled. "I don't blame you."

"Those kids love mac and cheese. How much of that crap can a person eat?"

"That depends. The domestic mages here make a killer mac and cheese."

"Yeah, because they make it with real cheese. It's creamy *and* stringy. I'm not sure what the crunchy stuff is on the top, but it's fantastic."

"Sure beats the noodles and powder that come in the narrow box."

I nodded. "But the kids love it. If it's not that, it's frozen chicken nuggets or cheese pizza. Trying to get those kids to eat something decent like a roast or a good stew is an uphill battle. Since Kat is helping Jeff at the rental store, it's not like she has a lot of time to make multiple meals."

"Make what you want. If the kids won't eat it, they'll be hungry. They'll learn eventually."

I sighed. "That's easier said than done. You underestimate the persistence of children. They will stick to their guns for days and yell and scream all the while. It's hard not to give in just to shut them up."

"They know exactly what they're doing."

"Maybe they do. Maybe they don't. It can be exhausting."

Hans shrugged. "Don't take my advice. I've never had kids. I was raised in a very strict household. My grandfather never tolerated any whining."

"How did he stop it?" I asked.

"He stared at me. He cracked his belt. Never hit me with it, but I knew he could."

I chuckled. "You were afraid of him."

"Sure. But sometimes fear is a good start. I learned later that everything he did for me was for my own good. I also knew he'd never actually hurt me. At some point, I can't say when, I replaced that fear with respect. Then, he didn't need to threaten me with his belt. He didn't have to yell or punish me."

I scratched my head. "Sometimes I wonder if the older generation just had a special touch. Or maybe we just look back at it different when things were just as chaotic for them as it is for us."

Hans smirked. "You *are* the older generation."

"Shut up."

Hans laughed. "Well, it's true. You are literally the same age that my father would be if he was still alive."

The door clicked and Evander let Elijah out. My son had the widest smile on his face.

"Why don't you show your father what we practiced?" Evander asked, rustling his fingers through Elijah's long, shaggy brown hair.

"Check this out!" Elijah ran into the room and grabbed a bottle of water from a cabinet. He unscrewed the cap. He held out his free hand with his palm pointed up and his fingers extended.

Two small semi-translucent portals formed above his hands about two feet apart. Elijah took his bottle of water and poured it into the bottom portal. The water flowed through the portal and out of the top one until it formed a constant stream of water between the two.

"That's pretty cool!" I exclaimed.

"Now watch this." Elijah leaned his head in and took a swig of water. "You can drink from it. You can also wash your hands." He put his hands in the stream of water. "If we had soap, which I know I'm *supposed* to use, it would work great!"

Hans grinned. "You could pee into it, too, you know."

Elijah laughed. "If I was going to do that I wouldn't make a never-ending stream. I'd put the other side in the toilet. That way I could pee anywhere and I wouldn't have to worry about dealing with the bathroom."

I tilted my head. "You'd still have to wash your hands."

Hans smiled. "You could poop in one and drop it on someone's porch."

"Don't give him any ideas!" I shouted.

Elijah grinned. "We could do that to the bad guys!"

I smiled. "I don't think dropping deuces on our enemies' porches is the way to defeat the enemy. Besides, son, they have gate mages, too. And they've already shown that they are willing to drop things a lot more dangerous than turds through them."

Elijah nodded. "Like bombs."

"It's one reason why your specialization is so important," Evander said. "If the enemy attacks us that way, gate mages might be our best chance to save us. If they drop a bomb on our headquarters, a good gate mage could send it away before it goes off."

I nodded. "Ideally dropping it somewhere safe. Where no one will get hurt."

Elijah pressed his lips together. "If we did it right, we could set up the portals to send any bombs they dropped right back through their own portal. Sort of like how I just did that with the water."

I chuckled. "That's not a bad idea. Is that doable, Evander?"

Evander nodded. "Technically, it is. But the only way to really pull it off would be to cloak our portals. Not impossible, but it requires using some good illusion magic alongside the creation of gates. There's also a downside to it."

"What is that?" Hans asked. "Sounds like a good plan to me."

Evander shook his head. "We don't know *where* the enemy might be sending them from. It was long before my time, but I know my history. The Axis mages often operated in the middle of populated areas, the basements of schoolhouses or hospitals, for that very reason."

I sighed. "Using innocent people as shields."

Evander nodded. "That's always been the advantage the Axis had over us. We have a conscience. They're also willing to use our conscience against us."

Elijah tugged my arm. "According to Professor P-Dick, virtue is never a weakness. A good conscience can make friends and allies. It's a stronger play."

I chuckled. "What did you call the professor?"

Elijah smiled wide. "P-Dick."

I snickered. "His name is Professor Pritchard."

"Right. Like P-Richard. P-Dick. That's what all the kids call him when he isn't around."

The corners of my mouth ached from trying to force myself not to laugh. "You should try to be respectful of your teacher, son."

Elijah raised an eyebrow. "You call him Professor Poppycock! How is that any different?"

Hans nudged me in the ribs. "Your son has a point."

I shook my head and chuckled. "You're too much like your father, son. I always had authority issues."

"Am I punk rock like you and Jessie used to be, Dad?"

I chuckled. "I suppose, in a way, you are."

CHAPTER THREE

Elijah had something going on every evening during the week. He had mage studies every Monday, Wednesday, and Friday. On Tuesdays and Thursdays, he had Taekwondo class. When my two littles got to an age where they wanted to get involved in things, especially if they manifested, Kat and I were going to have to figure out how to divide and conquer. I couldn't predict if all my boys would have the same interests. They were different enough and I expected they wouldn't. Kat and I were hardly the first parents in history who struggled to manage their children's schedules, and the only thing I knew for sure was that as busy as I was at the moment, it was the easiest it was ever going to be. Unless, of course, we ended the war with the Axis *before* my other kids got involved in extracurriculars.

As it was, I couldn't remember the last time I'd had any actual free time. I usually started each morning at AAA Tool Rental. I made sure everything was good to go for the day. Once the kids were off to school, Kat came and picked up the slack and worked with Jeff—our store manager—and our other employees until the kids got out. Jeff closed the store every day. I was glad I had someone working for me I could trust. He also knew about my mage responsibilities and understood why I couldn't work from open to close.

After Kat arrived each day, I did a variety of things. Some days, I trained early with Nigel. Usually, though, on days when Elijah had class or training, I worked with Nigel at that time. On other days, I spent time recruiting some of the American mage families. They weren't all on board with the alliance, but the ability to give their children a basic education in the specializations had an appeal. About half of the families were on board with the alliance. Half the rest supported our efforts but weren't directly involved. Only about a quarter of the mages opposed our efforts. Their complaints were the same: why work with the Brits, who'd operated a secret underground academy for decades and never invited us to participate? I suspected they simply didn't want to get involved in the conflict. They had lives of their own. Most of them had seen a taste of what Hana was capable of when she emerged at Gregory Park, but they were in denial about the prospect of another Arcane War.

When I wasn't engaging those families, I was meeting with the leaders of the alliance. We discussed strategies and received reports. We had dozens of gate mages, but only three empaths. Rose wasn't in a condition to help alone, but Jessie and Mary accompanied the gate mages as they scouted the world. The gate mages took them to various locations where we suspected Hana might be operating, and the empaths scanned the area, listening in on the thoughts of mages in the area, trying to pick up any intelligence that might be actionable.

Hana's empath, the infamous Goebbels, was a master propagandist. He'd used his skills as an empath during the prior Arcane Wars to recruit a sizable army loyal to the Axis cause. What was their cause? Hana told Hans exactly what she intended to do—she wanted to take over the mage world *and* the human world, and give Hans the opportunity to rule at her side. Hana had been dead for twenty years. Her aspirations were warped by years of communing with the darker depths of the arcane wells, and she intended to make up for all the years she'd missed in Hans' life by giving him the world.

Hans wasn't interested. He told her as much, but that didn't dissuade her in the least. Since Hana could wield almost every mage specialty, and even had abilities drawn from the darkest part of the wells that no mage had ever manifested before, there was no telling what she might do next.

Would she resurrect more Axis mages who fought in the Arcane Wars? Would she recruit modern-day mages? She'd probably do both. On top of all of that, we weren't sure if she could raise mages we'd already eliminated. Could she use necromancy to resurrect the same Axis mages twice? If someone was raised through necromancy, they came back different, with their minds bent and their powers unpredictable. If they came back a second time, they might emerge worse than before. It meant we couldn't make any progress in the long-term unless we could figure out how to cut Hana off from the wells. We needed to separate her from her source of power. The problem was that we didn't know a good way to do that, and she hadn't shown herself once over the last several months.

Kat texted me before we left to ask if I could pick up some food from the alliance cafeteria to bring home. I was glad to comply, and the domestic mages who ran the cafeteria were always happy to provide. It meant no mac and cheese. Even with the beanie-weenies added for protein, I wasn't sure my gut could handle it for the third time in the last couple of weeks.

Elijah and I stopped by the cafeteria, and the mages prepared a nice casserole for us. Plenty of vegetables with the secret sauce that allowed us to get them into the children's stomachs: lots of cheese.

They whipped the whole thing up in less than ten minutes. All we had to do once we got home was pop it in the oven for half an hour. I texted Kat to start preheating the oven to 350 as Elijah climbed into the passenger side of my truck.

Elijah had a small rubber ball that he was using to practice his gates, sending it through one to another. As I drove, he duplicated his double-gate routine and dropped his ball inside. He watched as it fell repeatedly between his gates. He was really taking to all of this, and he enjoyed it. Few things give a parent more satisfaction than seeing one of their children find a passion and not only have success with it but derive happiness from it.

Like most kids, Elijah had his quirks. As an older brother, he liked to pick on his siblings. Nothing unusual about that. The littles gave it as good as they got it. Kat and I rarely intervened. We'd had to learn that when kids tattle on each other, the worst thing you can do is take sides. There was almost always enough blame to go around. Unless someone was going to get hurt, it was usually best to let the boys sort things out. If Kat and I ever got involved, we couldn't take sides. Most of the time, it was impossible to know which boy carried the lion's share of the blame. If we had to intervene, it meant everyone involved was going to pay the price. The most common penalty? Lost screen time. It was what going to my room was when I was a kid. That didn't work with them, but take away their YouTube or their Nintendo? That was how they knew we were serious.

Elijah watched his ball pass between his portals. He swiped his hand between, trying to miss the ball every time it dropped. It was funny how the portals maintained their position in the truck, and didn't get left behind on the road. They traveled with us. I didn't know the physics behind it, but it probably had something to do with relative momentum. Still, the occasional bumps we hit on the road sometimes spoiled Elijah's timing, and he had to scoop up his ball and try again.

When we got home, the first thing Elijah wanted to do was show his mother and brothers what he learned. He was proud of his progress, and he was right to be. I was grateful we had the alliance and the academy. I didn't have that advantage when I was a kid. The old academies had long since closed. We had occasional convocations where we learned our skills in an intensive format, but those had ended almost twenty years before in the wake of all the infighting and disagreements that boiled up after the Caedes incident. The problem with the convocation was that we often packed too much learning into a short time, so retention was an issue. We always took a few steps back between convocations despite getting older, despite some of us practicing more than others. With the academy, Elijah could grow his skills and get better consistently. He was also starting younger than I did. The sky was the limit in terms of what he might be capable of if he stuck to it and continued working hard to develop his gift.

The oven was ready to go when we got inside. I carried the casserole in, kissed Kat on the cheek before she put the food in the oven and watched Elijah pass his ball between portals.

Elijah's display initially fascinated Ezra and Elliot but they quickly lost interest. They were both eager to show me things they'd done while I was gone. Ezra was working on his letters. He showed me how he wrote a complete sentence in various colors of crayon at school, accompanied by a picture that was supposed to be a "dinasar" according to the caption above. Spelling wasn't a concern in kindergarten. He was sounding it out and doing his best. According to his teacher, correcting spelling at that age was counterproductive.

"That's awesome!" I exclaimed. "Can I put it on the fridge? I want to see it every time I get food!"

Ezra's lips stretched into a wide, toothy grin. He jumped up and down on his bare little toes as I carried his picture to the fridge and stuck it to the front with a magnet.

Elliot took me over to see the small house he built with magnetic blocks. We didn't have magnetic blocks when I was a kid. It was brilliant. While it wasn't perfect, the magnets prevented the accidental disaster. Nothing was sure to set a three-year-old off more than if the block castle he was building collapsed before he was ready.

I kissed Elliot on the cheek. "I love it! Who is the king of the castle?"

"You are, Daddy! Mommy is the queen!"

"That must make you the brave knight, Sir Elliot!"

"I'm the bravest in the land! I slay dragons!"

"More than one? That *is* impressive. You must be a hero. I bet all the girls in the kingdom want to marry you!"

"Ew, Daddy! Girls are gross. Except for Mommy!"

I chuckled. Kat heard it and looked over and winked. "Just as it should be."

Of course, at various times, each of my boys had articulated their intention to marry their mother in the future. I was pretty sure they'd grow out of that notion in a few years. Soon, other girls would become "yum" and anything to do with mom and dad would be "ew."

A small portal formed over Elliot's castle. I reached out and caught the ball before it could crash the blocks to the floor. I stared daggers at Elijah from across the room.

He looked back at me with a wide grin on his face. I shook my head. "Be nice to your brothers."

Elijah shrugged. "What did I do?"

I rolled my eyes. "You know exactly what you were about to do. Stinker."

It was going to be a late dinner, so I started the nighttime routine and got the kids dressed for bed, left a glass of water on their nightstands, and pulled the shades closed in their rooms.

The casserole was fantastic. Even the kids loved it, and that was saying something. Half the time the kids said "ew" and turned their noses up at their plates before they took a single bite. With all the broccoli baked into the casserole, Elijah couldn't portal it into the yard without also sacrificing his cheese.

Our dinner conversation usually centered on what each of us did throughout the day. We all took turns sharing as we stuffed our faces. So long as no food went flying, the "no talking with your mouth full" rule was one we were willing to waive. We finished our meal and I helped Kat clean up before we took the kids to bed.

Ezra and Elliot were halfway there. They had nearly fallen asleep on the couch while Kat and I finished the dishes. Elijah was still watching someone with an incredibly annoying voice detail their Minecraft excursions on YouTube.

"All right, buddy," I said. "Turn it off. It's time for bed."

"I'm hungry!"

I stared at Elijah blankly. "We *just* had dinner."

"I know. But I'm hungry!"

"What do you want?"

"Food!"

I grunted. "Specifics, please."

"I don't know. I'm just hungry!"

"How about more of the casserole?"

"Yuck!"

"You liked it! You cleaned your plate."

"I want something else. I'm full of casserole. I'm hungry for something different."

"I don't think you understand how the stomach works."

"I'm hungry!" Elijah repeated himself just in case I hadn't received the message.

"How about carrot sticks?"

"Ew. Yuck."

"An apple?"

"Will you cut it up for me?"

I sighed. "Fine. But after that, you're going to bed."

He agreed, but I'd been through this routine before. He'd finish his apple and still complain he was hungry. At some point, after stuffing him with food for the last hour, he was going to have to go to bed no matter how hungry he claimed to be.

I wasn't sure if a gate mage could just portal food directly into his stomach. I wasn't going to suggest it. It was probably dangerous. Still, given how much he ate, it was almost like he had a portal in his stomach that made everything he ate disappear shortly after he swallowed it. He was a bottomless pit.

Eventually, we had to put our foot down. "You've had enough. It's time for bed."

I had to turn off the television. Telling him to do it usually took more effort and a lot of repetition. We took the kids back to bed. Kat had to lie with the little ones for a while to get them back to sleep.

After that, she usually joined me on the couch and we enjoyed a show together before we went to bed. On this particular night, however, I don't remember her coming out. I woke up a few hours later and she was already in bed. It had been a long day. Every day was long, given all I had to do. I shuffled my feet and crawled into bed next to Kat. I only had a few hours left before I had to get up and do it all over again.

CHAPTER FOUR

I woke up to the sound of *Adam's Song* by Blink-182. I swapped out my ringtone every couple of months, but I always stuck to the music of my youth. Back when punk rock was still punk rock —or so we thought—and when it took more talent and less auto-tune to produce an album. Hell, it was back when they actually produced albums. If I lamented one thing about the lives my sons were destined to live, it was that they'd never know the satisfaction of ripping the plastic off a new CD for the first time, popping it in your Discman, and putting your favorite songs on repeat.

I tossed my blanket off me and reached over to my nightstand.

"Who is it?" Kat asked.

I grunted. "Fucking Nigel."

"You're doing what with Nigel?"

I glared back at Kat before I answered the phone.

"Nigel, it's the middle of the night."

"Do you have your television on?"

My heart started to race. The last time someone called and

asked me that was early morning on the eleventh of September 2001.

"It's three in the morning. I don't have my television on."

"Turn it on."

I was already halfway to the living room. I didn't know what I was about to see, but I was already bracing myself. I grabbed my remote and turned on the television. Of course, it was on the YouTube app. Whatever Nigel wanted me to see was probably on the news. I switched over to a national news channel.

What I saw took my breath away.

An aerial view of Berlin, Germany. Half the city was in ruins. In the middle, a giant hole radiated violet energies. The caption at the bottom of the screen called it a "massive sinkhole." It was more than that. It was the largest breach into the arcane wells I'd ever seen.

"My God," I said.

"The center of the breach is even more concerning."

"I don't know my way around Berlin. What is it?"

"The breach is concentrated at the location of the Reich Chancellery. The Führerbunker."

I sighed. "I don't know German, but I'm guessing that's the bunker where Hitler died?"

"It is."

"Hana must be behind this."

"Undoubtedly."

"Is she raising…you know…"

"We're not sure. Keep watching."

I rubbed my eyes. I stared at the television screen as two dark and wispy forms escaped the breach. Two seconds later, three more emerged. "What are they?"

"We're not entirely sure. We've counted two hundred of them so far. The breach is also expanding. They might be ethereal creatures, entities of unknown power. They could be the souls of deceased mages, or even human impotens. Whatever they are, I don't think they're here to have tea and crumpets."

"I've never had a crumpet."

I could practically hear him roll his eyes. "I told you before, Thomas. It's griddle bread. That's beside the point. The amount of power Hana must've harnessed to do this is astronomical. With a breach like that, there's no telling what she might be able to do."

"Have we sent any scouts and gate mages to investigate?"

"Evander tried to portal there. He can't get any closer than a hundred kilometers away. It's like the energy blasting from the breach is silencing our abilities."

I gulped. "A hundred kilometers?"

"If the breach continues to expand, if the energy that's pouring out of that breach spreads, it might affect all of us."

"You're saying it could silence every mage in the world?"

"Perhaps not every mage. You and the other battlemages who've been to the ethereal realm might stand a chance."

I put my hand over my eyes. "We have to contain the breach before it gets that far. There aren't enough battlemages to take on Hana as it is. Especially if she and her Axis mages, whoever she might be pulling out of the arcane realms, can wield their powers unrestrained."

I felt a soft hand on the back of my neck. Kat stood next to me as we watched more ethereal shades escape the breach.

"There's no time to waste," Nigel said. "We need you here, and we need a plan."

"I'll be right there."

I hung up the phone, and Kat hugged me. More was happening than the threat to mages. How many lives were lost in the destruction? First responders were all over the scene. The news anchors were speechless. They were talking to a seismologist over the phone. I didn't have time to listen to his futile attempts to explain the phenomenon. Whatever he had to say wasn't accurate. Science couldn't explain what was happening. The world knew about mages. They chose to ignore us most of the time. They liked to pretend we were a minor force, a small community of wonder workers. For the most part, we didn't do much to dissuade that idea. Since the Arcane Wars, apart from the incident involving Caedes, we stayed out of the news.

Until now. Everything was about to change.

CHAPTER FIVE

I usually slept in my skivvies. No socks. I couldn't sleep with socks on. My sleeping habit had earned me the nickname "underwear man" among my kids. I slept with a t-shirt on, mostly because I didn't want my armpit stench getting on my sheets. I threw on a pair of cargo pants and a pair of tube socks and slipped on my boots. The one thing I'd learned the hard way was that when arcane bullshit was afoot, there was no telling when I might be whisked away via portal to confront the latest threat.

I snuck into the kids' rooms and gave them each one last kiss on their foreheads. They were fast asleep and wouldn't remember it. I'd remember it, no matter what. Hopefully, I'd be back soon. Given the gravity of the situation, I suspected it might be a while. I tried not to go there in my mind, but I always knew when I had to go into battle against dark mages that I could lose. I might not ever come back. It wasn't only when I was facing an arcane threat. Anytime I left the house, I tried to tell my family I loved them or leave them with a kiss in their sleep. Anything could happen. Life is precious. Family is everything.

I hurried back to my bedroom and grabbed my truck keys off my dresser, but a bright light flashed outside my bedroom door. I chuckled and tossed my keys back on my dresser. I wouldn't need them. I hurried out of the room.

Hans was waiting for me. "Ready to go?"

Kat grabbed my hand and pulled me into a deep kiss. "Do what you do best, babe."

I nodded at Hans. "Now, I'm ready."

Hans formed a portal and we both passed through it. We landed in the cafeteria at the alliance headquarters. We didn't have a good meeting room in the old closed-down hospital. They didn't have presentation rooms like they did on Grey's Anatomy where they'd scrutinize operating room mishaps. The best place we had to gather for a large-scale meeting was the cafeteria.

Generally, I hated meetings. We'd had more than a few after the Entente mages relocated to St. Louis. For a while, our meetings centered on dull topics like new curriculum development. Since most of the Entente mages lived in a world of their own, simple things like handling finances, how to behave in public, and where to buy toilet paper were major discussion topics.

This meeting was different. This was the sort of thing the Entente mages had prepared for their entire lives. Half of the Entente alliance had died when Hana Sato assaulted their underground base in London. A few families, largely those where gate magery dominated the gene pool, remained intact. Evander's entire family made it to St. Louis, but that was more the exception than the norm. Nearly everyone else had lost family members. Some were buried in the rubble. Others were executed by Hana and her necromantic sorcerers the moment the gate mages evacuated them to the surface. Those who didn't lose family still lost people close to them. The Entente chambers might have sheltered most of the mages there from the real world, but they also bound them together. Everyone who lived there was family, by blood or otherwise.

It was the middle of the night, but every eye in the room was glued to the flatscreen television on the wall. When I appeared, I received little more than a few glances and nods before people returned their focus to the broadcast. The looks on the mages' faces reflected concern, worry, and fear, but also anger and determination.

Nigel grabbed my arm and pulled me aside. "Leadership needs to get on the same page. We need to discuss our next steps."

I nodded and followed Nigel down a hall to what used to be the hospital chapel. Nigel represented the battlemages. Evander was there as the leader of the gate/portal mages. Mary was there with Jessie, two of our three empaths.

Professor Pritchard, a.k.a. Poppycock, a.k.a. P-Richard, a.k.a. P-Dick, was also there to provide some historical perspective. He and Mary were both a lot older than they looked. The Entente mages had an elective process that allowed mages to extend their lifespans. It was reportedly a very painful experience and wasn't always successful. It involved using arcane power to lengthen someone's telomeres. A lot of risk was involved, and it could kill someone outright if their body didn't respond to the process as expected. Thus, there weren't a lot of mages who chose to undergo the procedure. Still, a few did.

Although Pritchard and Mary didn't appear to be any older than me, the truth was that they had been in their forties during the Arcane Wars, when they endured the procedure. That put them each somewhere in the neighborhood of a hundred and twenty years. They had lived through the Arcane Wars. They knew the Axis strategies and the ways the alliance fought against them in the past, what worked and what didn't work. They had a lot of insight gleaned not from history books, but from real experience. They say that the value in studying history is that we might not repeat the errors of the past. We didn't have to rely on studying the past, though. We had real witnesses of the former wars who'd experienced it.

Another television mounted to the wall in the former chapel was broadcasting the newscast. The volume was muted, as there wasn't much the talking heads could say that would help us discern what was happening. Still, the images on the screen spoke volumes about how the situation was evolving.

"What are everyone's thoughts on the situation?" I began. "Is there anything we can do?"

"The location of this event is not a mistake," Pritchard replied. "Hana Sato is making a statement. The Führerbunker is symbolic for the failure of the Axis powers—including the Axis mages whose efforts piggy-backed on those of the Third Reich."

"It may be more than that," Mary pointed out. "Hana Sato still has Goebbels. There was a lot of conversation at the time that I'd discerned involving experiments to invest the Führer with arcane abilities."

I snorted. "Is that even possible? To change a non-mage into a mage? I thought our abilities were inherited."

Mary shrugged. "There were experiments."

"It should not come as a surprise," Pritchard added. "The Nazis experimented on human beings in the camps. This is not news. However, most of the attempts to create human-animal chimeras occurred at the embryonic level. I suspect they did the same in attempts to normalize the occurrence of the mage genes. I'm not aware of any experiments, however, that involved attempts to force genetic alteration on adults."

"That's not strictly true," Mary suggested. "We know that the genetic component of magery is not detectable by conventional scans or biology. It's an ethereal organ of sorts, something affixed to the spirit of a human being that is inherited from one's parents. Impotens are those born to mage families who for whatever reason didn't receive that genetic trait. They had no ethereal organ and no capacity to access arcane power."

Nigel cleared his throat. "Impotens technically applies to any human who cannot access arcane power. Though most people not born to a mage family aren't familiar with the term."

Mary extended her index finger. "Again, nothing about that is untrue. However, there were discussions at the time about transplanting the ethereal organ from mage prisoners or those with an arcane heritage in the concentration camps into those whose other genetic traits were deemed most desirable."

I tilted my head. "If the organ responsible for our abilities is ethereal, how could it be surgically transplanted?"

Evander shook his head. "Not surgically. Not through scalpels and anesthesia. Through portals, carefully cast from one person into another."

"Precisely," Mary agreed. "It's believed that there are certain genetic traits that correspond with the likelihood that a mage will manifest. Nothing you'd recognize by observance, but nonetheless a part of the genome that often determines if a mage is likely to inherit abilities from one's parents. Theoretically, there are humans born to non-mage humans who might be more receptive to ethereal power if only they had the organ."

This sounded crazy. "We're still talking about an *organ,*" I stressed. "Is that something that can be fused to someone else's spirit?"

Mary shrugged. "I do not know the results of their experiments, but in theory, it's possible. We speak of it as an ethereal organ, but we know little about how it functions. It may be that a better analogy to biology is a parasite rather than an organ. A separate entity that latches itself to the human spirit at an ethereal level."

"Parasites? That doesn't sound good at all."

"It's a common misconception that parasites are all bad," Pritchard explained. "Some parasites have a symbiotic relationship with their hosts. They have measurable benefits. There are bacteria, for instance, that are independent of a host but provide a number of health benefits."

"Like probiotics," I suggested.

Pritchard nodded. "Precisely. It is an intriguing theory. Consider this. Even if it is not possible to use portal magery to transfer such a parasite from a mage to an impotens, if a deceased human soul enters the arcane realm, it's not unthinkable that one raised through necromancy might manifest powers that he or she never realized in life."

I rubbed my brow. "I'm not an especially religious man. Still, the immortality of the soul isn't out of the question. Hana's existence confirms as much. Do common humans go to the arcane realms when they die? Or do they go to some place more like heaven or hell?"

"The difference may merely be semantic," Mary offered. "Traditional religion might not ascribe arcane power to what they call heaven, but that doesn't mean arcane energy isn't a part of everyone's afterlife experience. It may simply be that arcane energy is to the dead what oxygen is to the living."

I shook my head. "So our working theory is that these dark figures escaping the breach might be human souls raised through Hana's necromantic power that might be mages their second time around?"

"It's conjecture," Nigel reminded us. "We should consider the possibility that any being we encounter raised by Hana might have powers we aren't aware of."

I took a deep breath and exhaled. "Hana was dead for nearly two decades. I'm guessing she knows a lot more about how any of that works than we do. That gives her an advantage. Regardless, even if these people are brought back to life, it doesn't help us figure out how to stop it. Our first priority should be to close the fissure. We can worry about whatever threats Hana unleashed on the world after that."

Jessie stepped forward. "Apologies, I know I don't know nearly as much about any of this as the rest of you. Even if we knew how to close a fissure of that magnitude, there's a lot we don't know about it. When we fought Caedes and worked to defeat the fiends his fissure released in the park, we managed to close it, but we played right into his hand by doing so. We only made him more powerful in our attempt to stop what he was doing. Is it really wise to do anything at all if we don't know exactly what we're facing, or what Hana's plans are regarding the fissure?"

Pritchard straightened his tie. "It's a fair point. However, our gate mages can't create portals there. It's not going to be easy to investigate without boots on the ground."

"Then the battlemages who can cast there, those of us who've been to the ethereal realm and have already shown an ability to harm Hana and her undead mages, need to investigate the situation," I concluded.

"We can't get you any closer than about a hundred kilometers from ground zero," Evander cautioned.

"Then get us as close as you can. Gate us several vehicles so we can drive there. We'll find out what we can."

Jessie looked uncomfortable. "Tommy, if you do that and you find yourself in a precarious situation, our gate mages won't be able to rescue you. You'll have to either fight or run."

"And without an empath, you won't have the advantage of discerning their intentions," Mary added.

I shrugged. "These are all mages like Hana, fully vested with dark power. Our empaths are already deaf to their thoughts."

"That's not necessarily true," Mary argued. "Since the fissure silences our abilities, Goebbels is free to use his influence in the area to recruit living mages. They may not be completely sold-out to the dark power. They probably aren't. If we could get into the area, there might still be a few things we could discern from the mage community in the region."

Pritchard looked thoughtful. "That might be the significance of the location. Berlin has always been home to a large mage population. While most of them do not embrace the Axis ideology, neither did the mages who Goebbels recruited to the Axis before. Remember, he is a master propagandist. Many good mages fell to his influence before. There's no reason to suspect the mages there today will be any more resistant to his propaganda than those before."

I cracked my knuckles. "If that's true, then if we can find Goebbels, eliminating him should be our first priority. Even before closing the fissure. Whether Hana is resurrecting the dead, recruiting living mages, or both, it's his influence that poses the greatest threat. So long as he's allowed to use his abilities to warp minds and recruit mages to his cause, the larger the army they'll be able to assemble against us."

"I agree," Mary said. "If you can take out Goebbels, Hana will have to be more cautious. There's no guarantee that anyone she resurrects, or any of the mages in the region, will take her side."

Nigel took a deep breath. "It's not ideal, but it may be the only way we can get to the bottom of what's going on. Jessie is right. Until we know exactly what we're facing, any grand efforts to stop it could be counterproductive."

"Do you agree with my proposal to eliminate Goebbels?" I pressed.

"If we can locate him, then yes. However, we must also take the opportunity to glean whatever we can about the situation. Eliminating Goebbels won't end the crisis. We'll still have a lot of work to do to stop Hana Sato." Nigel looked at me grimly. "However, taking him out would certainly throw a wrench in her plans. It may be our best move."

CHAPTER SIX

We had a company of roughly a hundred battlemages with the capacity to attack ethereal entities and those warped by dark magic like Hana and the soldiers she'd resurrected before. I made the mistake of calling us a battalion, but Nigel corrected me. We were too small to be considered a battalion. We were a company.

Whatever. I didn't have any military experience, and I wasn't hip on the lingo. Still, a hundred people, all needing vehicles so we wouldn't have to hoof it a hundred kilometers into Berlin, required a lot of gates and a suitable location where Hans and Evander could drop us.

We needed to leave sooner rather than later, but rallying so many people at once, ensuring everyone was dressed for the occasion and properly armed with their wands, took a little time. Nigel also wanted to call his contact in the British Parliament to inform him of our plan. The US government was more hands-off and generally followed the lead of their European allies. The fissure wasn't on US soil, so it wasn't their concern. Not yet, anyway.

Nigel insisted that it was best to communicate with the secular powers-that-be lest they get in our way. There were probably barricades in the area and soldiers evacuating the people. Not to mention, our vehicles had Missouri plates. We weren't street-legal, probably not even on the autobahns. I didn't have my passport on me, and I wasn't sure if the other battlemages *had* passports.

While Nigel made his calls, I outlined the plan with the rest of the alliance in the cafeteria. I dismissed the qualified battlemages to dress accordingly, grab their wands, and spend a moment with their families before we left.

The alliance wouldn't be left defenseless. There were plenty of battlemages besides all the domestic and gate mages, not to mention our two empaths, to hold down the fort. We didn't have any reason to believe Hana was concerned with our base of operations. She probably knew about us, and it wouldn't be hard for her to find us. A five-second trip to the region with Goebbels and she'd know where we were. Chances were good that at some point over the last several weeks, she'd done exactly that. The one thing you have to be prepared for when dealing with mages is the unexpected. Just because an enemy is focusing on the other side of the globe didn't mean they couldn't launch an assault somewhere else in a split second. No borders or boundaries could protect us. The same had applied to them as well—until now. This fissure effectively created a safe zone where our ability to counter Hana's efforts was limited.

I gave everyone two hours to get ready. Maybe that was too much time, but I wasn't going to lead a bunch of battlemages into a precarious situation without giving them enough time to see their families. It was also worth taking a bit more time to evaluate how the situation on the ground was evolving.

If I knew the situation was static, if nothing was going to change, I'd have tried to get a little rest myself. I remembered what it was like when I first turned the television on that September morning in 2001, when only one tower had been hit. Before the second plane struck the other one, I'd had a gut feeling that it wasn't over. I didn't know what was coming, but I sensed *something* more was going to happen. I had the same gut feeling now as I watched the newscast from Berlin.

It was just a matter of time before the field reporter would broadcast from the scene. Reporters were like that. They thought broadcasting in the middle of a dangerous situation gave their reports more credence. I couldn't count the number of times I'd seen reporters standing in hurricane-force winds with debris flying behind them, trees bent almost horizontal, while they screamed into the microphone just to tell everyone the obvious: the winds were really bad and everyone brighter than the reporter should evacuate.

I sat next to Jessie on the edge of one of the cafeteria tables. She held the remote and turned up the volume as the in-studio newscast broke away to a reporter in the field.

"Predictable," I scoffed.

Jessie snickered. "Dumb, dumb, dumb. They have no idea what they're dealing with."

"To be fair, we aren't entirely sure what we're facing, either."

"At least we aren't entertaining the possibility of a seismic event here. What earthquake ever released dark energies from the ground? What do they think it is? Natural gas?"

"There are a few fires in the area. No clue how any of them started, but if that was natural gas the entire area would go boom."

"There's nothing natural in the Earth's crust that looks anything like that. There's no record of volcanic activity there. How long do you think it will take before they consider the truth?"

I shook my head. "They'll look for every other explanation first. It's been so long since mages made the news, and never has anything remotely close to this happened, that they won't admit it until it smacks them upside the face."

Jessie's eyes widened. "Did you see that?"

"See what?"

Jessie paused the broadcast and set it back about ten seconds. "Look just over the reporter's right shoulder."

Jessie let it play and paused it again at the right moment. "That's it!"

I gulped. There was a man in what looked like an old SS uniform, complete with a red band on his arm, walking past in the rubble behind the reporter. He only appeared for a half-second before he disappeared. "Holy shit. I seriously doubt that Nazi cosplay is a thing in Berlin."

Jessie shook her head. "Definitely not. That's the real thing."

"Look at his eyes. They're black like coal."

"Dark arcane power," Jessie whispered. "It appears our suspicion was right. Those black figures emerging from the fissure were human souls."

"How did he get a body like that?" I asked. "Before, Hana was raising the dead at gravesites. She needed their bodies or at least something of their remains to do it."

"We saw her raise someone from ashes once before. It doesn't take much."

"Hana could have brought a large quantity of ashes to the site. Perhaps that's what she's been doing all this time when we didn't see her. Hand-selected persons she wanted to bring back from the dead. The breach gave her the power to raise them all at once."

Jessie stared at the freeze-frame of the ominous SS figure. "It makes sense. When she was going from cemetery to cemetery before we were on her tail. She was waiting until she was sure she could resurrect a large enough force to challenge us."

"This changes nothing. We still have to eliminate Goebbels. If Hana recruits the living mages in Berlin, it will give her an even greater advantage. If we can take Goebbels out of the picture and rally those mages to our side rather than hers, we might stand a chance."

"Those mages still won't have any power in the area. No more than our mages do. Not unless you can do for them what you did for our battlemages and bring them to the ethereal realm."

I nodded. "That might be true. Still, if we can get them away from the city, perhaps there's something we can do to stop the fissure from spreading. At the very least, even if they are powerless, it's better than having them vested with dark arcane power and fighting against us."

Jessie snapped a picture of the freeze-frame and resumed the broadcast. We watched every frame waiting for more long-dead Axis enemies to appear. The field reporter didn't talk for long. They returned to the studio and the bird's-eye view of the fissure. No one mentioned the figure in the background. Had they missed it? The SS soldier *had* only appeared for a split second before he moved out of the shot. If we saw it, though, surely we weren't the only ones.

Nigel joined us and sat beside me. "I just got off the phone with the British Embassy in Berlin."

"What are they saying?"

He scratched his head. "I'm not sure you'd believe it if I said it."

I smirked. "Given the fact that we just saw what looked like an SS soldier in the background on live television, I'm not sure there isn't much I wouldn't believe."

Nigel pressed his lips together. "That tracks with what I'm hearing from the embassy."

"What are they saying?" Jessie asked.

"A contingency of soldiers wearing SS uniforms and a man purporting to be Hitler himself appeared in the Federal Chancellery two hours ago. He gave the chancellor twenty-four hours to turn over the reins of the government or he would take it by force."

"They reported this to the British Embassy?"

Nigel nodded. "If someone appeared by a portal who looked

like a man who has supposed to have been dead for the better half of the last century, the most despised dictator of history, and mages were clearly involved, it makes sense that the Brits would be included in the conversation. The chancellor knew about our Entente chambers. He didn't know that Hana Sato had already launched the first attack in this Arcane War, but he hoped we could help."

I sighed. "Another Arcane War. I was hoping to avoid that."

Nigel shook his head. "The war started the moment Hana Sato portaled a bomb into our chambers. There's no turning back now."

I grabbed Wand from my pocket and twirled him in my fingers. "One thing we know for sure. The longer we wait, the more powerful Hana and the Axis will become."

"We are the only real hope to stop a full-scale World War. If we cannot stop the mages, suffice it to say that the British government is not inclined to let a resurrected Hitler get a foothold. If we do not stop them, they are prepared to unleash the full force of their military capacity on Berlin."

I cleared my throat. "The *full* force?"

Nigel nodded.

"That means nuclear weapons, right?" Jessie demanded.

Nigel stood. He pulled his wand from his pocket. "They didn't say. I suspect that's not off the table. The British Embassy is preparing a convoy outside Berlin to take us in. We won't need to bring vehicles with us."

CHAPTER SEVEN

Briefing the battlemages was difficult. This whole leadership thing was fine when we were in the heat of the moment, a small group gathered in my living room making plans to take down a dark mage. Outlining legit battle plans to a group of more than a hundred, many of whom were better trained than I was, was downright intimidating.

I was in charge of the alliance for one reason: I got a little lucky and managed to save half the alliance from complete extinction. Most of the battlemages were sent to a glacier in the Arctic courtesy of Ichabod—a gate mage who'd been an Axis spy during the Arcane Wars but decided to blend in when his side failed. He didn't reveal his true colors until Hana emerged. The only reason he didn't send the battlemages to the moon, or the bottom of the ocean, was because if he killed them directly it would taint his magic and he was hoping to resume his role as a spy. I figured him out. He'd exercised a loophole by sending the battlemages to a hostile environment without a way out. That meant his magic didn't kill them. The elements would have killed them if we didn't find them in time.

My grandfather had been one of the founders of the Entente

alliance, and Nigel believed I'd inherited a unique ability from him, a gift for insight and wisdom, an ability to see connections that others missed. I wasn't convinced. If anything, my gift was that when shit hit the fan, my mind went into overdrive. I knew lives were at stake. I put the pieces together the best I could and had a few good guesses. Lives were saved. Now, I was the de facto "leader."

Jessie knew I had doubts. I couldn't hide anything from her. She was an empath, after all. She believed that my doubts were more reason I should lead. The best leaders don't seek power, she insisted. They rise to the occasion when they're needed. It was a nice sentiment, but it didn't do much for my internal doubt. It was one thing when I was in my twenties, with a confidence that bordered on arrogance, to stop an old friend turned dark mage and serial killer. To go to war with Hitler, though? To stop another World War? Knowing that the only way to stop a war was to win a mage war that had already begun? It was a huge burden for a man who rented tools for a living and hadn't engaged in much battle strategy outside the domains of *Call of Duty* or *Stratego*.

It wasn't exactly a formal presentation. We didn't have time to put together a PowerPoint, and if we had the time I still wouldn't have. I sucked at PowerPoint and there's nothing worse than sitting through one of those presentations. Jessie figured out how to screen-share her phone to the television, and she showed the picture of the soldier behind the reporter. I asked Nigel to relay what he'd learned when he spoke to his contact at the British Embassy in Berlin.

After he finished, I stepped up again. "They're going to take us into the city with a military convoy. I don't suspect Hana Sato will show her face. If she does, you know what to do. We're reasonably sure that Goebbels is somewhere nearby. He must be eliminated at all costs. We don't know what exactly we're going to encounter once we get to Berlin. If we don't find Goebbels, we take out any resurrected dark mages we find. The only thing we know for sure about how to destroy a fissure into the arcane wells is to eliminate the portal mage responsible. Let's hope the trail of resurrected Nazis leads us to her *and* Goebbels."

One of the battlemages raised his hand. I was awful with names. They all knew mine, of course. I was one person. How was I supposed to remember the names of a hundred people? I pointed at him to acknowledge his question. "Go ahead."

"Hana is a gate mage. If she knows we're coming she'll flee. Gate mages are difficult to kill."

I nodded. "And if Goebbels is with her, she'll take him with her. We'll need to separate them."

"And how exactly are we supposed to do that?"

I took a deep breath. My hands were shaking. I tried my best to stop it.

Jessie grabbed my hand and a wave of calm swooped over me. She'd picked up a few skills since she'd been training with Mary. Settling my emotions and giving me a sense of calm was one of her many gifts that I suspected I'd need again. Unfortunately, she couldn't come with us.

I took a deep breath. "We don't know. We can't make a plan when we don't know the situation. I'll simply say this: if anyone gets a clear shot at Goebbels, take it before Hana can intervene. Don't hesitate."

Nigel nodded. "If he's out of the picture, it will buy us time. You all know the history. You've taken the classes. He can affect people's thoughts. That means he's not only a threat to recruit other mages, but he may attempt to infiltrate your minds as well."

Mary stepped up in front of Nigel. "The thing you must know about how empath magery works is that we can't force a thought into someone's mind unless they respond to it, interact with it. If you have any thoughts at all that you think might be coming from Goebbels, ignore them. Don't even try to argue with him."

"You've been trained for this," Nigel assured everyone.

"Everything you've practiced your whole life has been for this moment."

"Think about your families," I added. "I know a lot of you lost family members in the attack on the chambers."

"Fight for them," Mary suggested. "Discipline your minds. Rage is a volatile emotion. It makes you more vulnerable to Goebbels' influence. Fight for their memories. For what they and you stand for. That will engender resolve. Resolve is like a fire-wall. An empath can't manipulate it. It will chase him out of your mind."

I nodded. "Right. What she said."

Jessie chuckled.

I was making a fool out of myself. I was trying to guide these people, but I didn't know what the hell I was doing. I remembered what I'd learned about leadership from my courses. It was better to be honest with oneself about one's weaknesses and to trust those who had the skills to do what you couldn't. Leaders don't have to be the most skilled person in every discipline. They lead because they have a vision and can inspire others to contribute their talents to the cause.

I took a deep breath. "The truth is, I've fought in some battles with dark mages before, but you are all better trained than I am. You've been preparing for this your entire lives. When I brought you all here I hoped it would give all of us a fresh start. I also knew it was only a matter of time before Hana made her next move.

"A lot of people like to talk about making history. What we do today and in the days ahead might not ever make the history books. If Hana succeeds, however, it will change the course of the future. A future we are fighting to preserve for our families, for all mages, and for all of humanity. We have a unique chance today to close a dark chapter in what could become history before it starts.

"We don't know what we're going to face. We don't know

where Hana is. We don't know where Goebbels is. We don't even know if the men brought back from the grave might have powers they didn't have in their natural lives. What we do know is what we can do. I haven't known any of you very long. Hell, I can't remember half of your names. But I've seen in each of your eyes a commitment and a resolve, a courage and a strength, a light illuminated by arcane power that will shine our way forward."

My speech wasn't met with raucous applause. I was hardly Mel Gibson's William Wallace. Maybe if we were on a battlefield and the enemy was on the other side, if we knew exactly what we were facing, the response would have been more exuberant.

We weren't sure if we were going into the battle of our lives, or if we'd end up wandering around an evacuated city and find nothing. We didn't know if we'd face the Axis mages or ethereal beings like the fiends we faced before. Did Hana and her allies know we were coming?

With Goebbels at her side, she'd see us coming. She could strategize. We'd enter the city blind, without a clue what we were facing or where our enemies were hiding. We had every disadvantage. The problem was that the further the energy released from the fissure spread, the more territory our enemies would claim. Would our enemies lure us in and fight or would they hide as long as they could, bide their time so that the energy could expand, so more spirits or beings from the wells might emerge to join their cause?

All we could do was wait for Nigel to get the call. Once the convoy was ready, Evander, Hans, and a few other gate mages would send us to Germany.

While we waited, the domestic mages prepared a meal. It was early morning, about six o'clock. It was early afternoon in Berlin. Hopefully, we'd get there with enough sunlight left to make some progress before nightfall.

The domestic mages served up just about any breakfast food one could want. Bacon and eggs. Biscuits and gravy. Oatmeal.

Who the hell would choose oatmeal? If it was about whatever tasted best, no one. We needed energy. We needed our strength. That's what I chose.

Everyone had their fill and finished breakfast just about the time Nigel got the call. The gate mages formed their portals, a half-dozen different gateways to take us all to the outskirts of Berlin.

CHAPTER EIGHT

The convoy was waiting for us when we arrived. So far as inconspicuous locations went, this was about as unlikely as it got. It was a farm somewhere at least a hundred kilometers outside Berlin.

I didn't know what kind of farm it was. I'd lived in suburbs and cities my entire life. The best I could say was that they grew stuff. I wasn't even sure if it was human stuff. Their crops might have been for feeding animals. The property was expansive, and I didn't see any farmhouses or structures aside from a few modest barns in view. I wasn't sure if it was intentional, but it struck me as a sound strategy. While Goebbels might sense our arrival, the further we were from wherever he was, the less likely it was he'd pick us up. Usually, an empath had to focus if he or she was surveying the presence of mages in a region. Since the Axis mages wouldn't know where we were coming from, it put them at a slight disadvantage. It was probably the only disadvantage they'd have in this conflict, but it was something.

I wasn't any hipper on military terminology than I was on farming. I wasn't sure what the technical term was for the transport vehicles they had lined up, but they were army green, had large tires, box-shaped cabs, and long beds covered in canvas. Each truck could carry about twenty of our mages, and there were six trucks in total.

The vehicles were on loan from the German government. The British Embassy must not have had the vehicles necessary for our transport. Nigel handled the conversation with the representative from the British Embassy and the representative from the German military who would be accompanying us on our approach.

We didn't waste any time and boarded the trucks. Nigel joined me in one of them, and it was a good chance to find out if he'd learned anything when he spoke to his embassy contact.

"Anything new?" I asked.

Nigel shook his head. "Not a lot. The fissure is expanding as we anticipated but they have no idea how far the range of its magic-neutralizing effects might be. It's wholly possible that the fissure will stop expanding at some point while whatever energies it's releasing continue pouring out and increase the area where our other mages can't cast."

I nodded. "That's to be expected. The fissure left behind when Hans made the mistake of trying to rescue Caedes, his father, was enough to pose a threat and that fissure wasn't a fraction of the size of the one I saw on television."

"There's no way to know how far the reach of the energies might spread," Nigel explained. "I don't see any reason why it wouldn't continue to grow indefinitely. The size of the fissure might only determine how rapidly it happens."

"It might not take long at all. Are there any more reports of SS soldiers or ethereal fiends? Anything else out of the ordinary?"

"There are a lot of reports. Everything is in such disarray right now, though, that they don't have an adequate assessment as to the accuracy of what's being reported. There are several sightings of SS officers, most of them with black holes for eyes, but so far there've only been sightings. There's no evidence that these reanimated soldiers are acting violently or communicating with people. All of what we know is compounded by the fact that the government is evacuating people from the area. That means fewer eyes on the ground. Fewer folks with cell phones and cameras to capture what they're seeing."

I pressed my lips together. "That's something I didn't think about. This is the twenty-first century. There must be cameras in the city, not to mention individuals capturing footage themselves. Has anyone checked social media?"

Nigel shrugged. "They didn't mention anything like that. My guess is that all of this has happened so fast that whatever data they have hasn't been seriously analyzed yet. Not to mention, it's hard to know if what people post on the Internet is real or not."

I pinched my chin. "That's true. There are always those out there who release fake content during events like this, knowing certain keywords are trending and people are searching for certain phrases. People are looking for views, likes, retweets, shares, or subscribes. Depending, of course, on which platform they're posting their footage to."

Nigel nodded. "That's probably true. Still, it wouldn't hurt to look at what's out there. We should be able to tell the difference between what's real and what isn't."

I pulled out my phone. It took me about two seconds to realize it was no use. "No service. We're too far away from civilization."

Nigel chuckled and grabbed his phone. "Won't be a problem for me."

"How do you have access?"

Nigel grabbed another small box from his pocket. "This connects to satellites. My phone connects to the device by Wi-Fi."

I huffed. "I had no idea things like that existed."

Nigel smirked. "We didn't see much action in the Entente chambers, but we were prepared in case we ever did." He studied his phone for a few minutes and grunted. "Nothing much helpful.

A lot of people freaked out. Several inaccurate conspiracies. What do you think the most frequent one is that I'm seeing?"

I shrugged. "Inside job by the government?"

Nigel chuckled and shook his head. "Aliens."

I rolled my eyes. "Of course. This might be easier if it were aliens."

"How do you figure?"

"Aliens might not know what we can do. A gate mage could send us on their ships. We could blast them to pieces and portal out of there."

"If a gate mage could get us inside. It's hard to portal inside of vessels without knowing what's inside. What if the aliens came from an environment where they breathed goo? We might tele-port inside and drown in it."

I snorted. "What aliens breathe goo?"

"I don't know. I've never met any aliens. That's the point. We wouldn't know any more about them than they would us."

I moved on. "What other theories are out there?"

"Some people think the violet energy pouring out of the hole is some kind of top-secret noxious gas stored underground by the Nazis."

"That's not an entirely irrational theory. It is centered on the Führerbunker."

Nigel continued scanning through various feeds on his phone. He saw something that made him narrow his eyes and show me his phone. Someone had posted on Twitter. She was evacuating her apartment and had caught a photo of a woman with long black hair walking the opposite way down the hall with three men in SS uniforms. One of the men, I suspected, was Goebbels. I couldn't see his face, but the back of his head suggested it might have been him. The other two men were younger. We couldn't see their eyes. If we could, I imagined they'd be dark as sin. Most of the responses ranged from "WTF" to accusing her of being tasteless and a fraud. There isn't a place in the world where you can walk around in an SS uniform and get away with it, and in Berlin, where the history hit so close to home, it was despicable to reveal Nazi sympathies. If the photo showed their faces, it may have elicited very different responses.

"Can you send her a DM? See if you can get an address."

Nigel took his phone back. "I had the same thought. It might take a little convincing. I don't know that I'd be willing to give a stranger my address. Especially with all the hate she's getting."

"If you can get her to respond, try to find out any other details. Did they enter another room? Were they saying anything she might remember?"

Nigel typed a message to the woman on his phone. I didn't bother him. I imagined he was telling her that he believed her, that he suspected those four people were responsible for what was happening, and that he was working with the authorities to track them down. Then again, perhaps he took a different approach. So long as he got actionable intelligence from her, it didn't matter. At the very least, it gave us a place to begin our search.

The convoy was moving. The roads were bumpy at first, but when they smoothed out, our pace picked up. We were probably a couple of hours away. We couldn't see outside the convoy, but I heard a few sirens and horns honking and I envisioned bumper-to-bumper traffic. People were evacuating Berlin en masse.

Nigel's eyes were glued to his phone. He started typing.

"Get a response?"

Nigel nodded. "She's a bit hesitant but I think she'll talk."

I sat and twiddled my thumbs. Nigel stood and approached the rear of the transport. He leaned outside and took a photo of the convoy running behind us. Then, he took another with himself in the photo holding up three fingers.

"What are you doing?"

"Giving her proof. The convoy shows I'm with the military.

The three fingers is what she asked me to show in the picture to prove I was there."

I grinned. "That's smart. Was that your idea or hers?"

"I asked her how I could prove myself to her. I suggested I send a picture of our convoy moving toward Berlin. She insisted I add verification."

"Is she responding?"

"I just sent the photos. I'm sure she will soon."

A few seconds later, a wide grin split Nigel's face. "Jackpot. Got the address."

"Any other details she can offer?"

Nigel shook his head. "She already said that they weren't talking. She saw them leave one room and enter another one. It made her nervous that they'd go to her apartment after she left."

"It sounds like Hana and her friends were looking for something."

"They might be long gone by now. The photo was taken a couple hours ago. Still, it's the best lead we have."

"If we go there, perhaps we can search the apartments ourselves. We might be able to figure out what they were looking for. It could give us an idea what they're trying to do."

CHAPTER NINE

As the caravan entered the affected area, we felt a distinct shift in the energy. A sense of unease hung in the air. It felt almost like it did when I was in the ethereal mist back at Gregory Park, battling the fiends, trying to save Hans and take down Caedes.

Nigel pulled out his wand and cast a saber. We weren't going to fight in the truck, but he was testing it to make sure his magic still worked. I followed suit and did the same. The *Star Wars* geek within me hoped our sabers would turn red in this environment, but they still glowed blue. We were Jedi knights, not Sith lords. It was the one detail that was off during my Darth Vader cosplay attempt before. It was probably for the best. Despite my Sith Lord fantasy that one day I might become Darth Tom, it was Hana and her minions who were tapping into the dark part of the wells. We were the light-side arcane battlemages. If I couldn't be a Sith Lord, being a Jedi Knight wasn't so bad.

Nigel showed me his phone. He was streaming a news broadcast. The bird's-eye view of the scene was flickering. "What is happening?"

I tilted my head. "I'm not sure."

A blast of dark magic flashed from the fissure, and the camera went out. About two seconds later, Nigel's phone died and the vehicles all stopped.

Nigel frowned. "That blast must've been like an electro-magnetic pulse."

"It neutralized pretty much anything that operates on electricity within the area."

"We're going to have to walk the rest of the way in."

I stood. "All right, everyone. Grab your things. We're making the rest of the trip on foot."

Everyone disembarked from our transport, and I ran to the other vehicles. The opposite lane was stuck. The people evacuating the city were going to have to leave their cars behind.

I pulled Nigel aside. "Please tell me you remember where that apartment is."

Nigel nodded. "Thankfully, I committed the address to memory."

"Do you know your way around Berlin?"

"Not really."

"How much good is an address going to do if we don't know where we're going?"

Nigel sighed. "That's a bloody good point."

I rubbed my brow. Then it dawned on me. If I were ten years younger, it probably never would have occurred to me. "Check the trucks. See if any of them have maps in the front."

"Right. Brilliant."

Nigel tapped on the driver's side window of one of the transport trucks. The driver couldn't lower his window, so he opened the door slightly, and a few seconds later Nigel appeared with a folded-up map.

"Looks like we're doing this old-school," I quipped.

"Ever use one of these things?"

I laughed. "I'm not that young. Maybe the driver can help us find the address."

"Right!"

Nigel returned to the truck to chat with the driver.

"Got it," Nigel said as he walked back over to me. "The problem is now that we're on foot, it will be dark before we reach the city."

"Where are we? Can you show me on the map?"

Nigel held out the map. We were still almost fifty kilometers out. If we could keep up a pace of about one kilometer every ten minutes, it would be well past dark when we got there.

I sighed. "And we'll be exhausted when we arrive without a place to crash if we need it."

Nigel nodded. "That also presumes we don't run into any trouble between here and there."

I scratched my head. "We could only hope we'd be that lucky."

"My thoughts exactly. Do you think it's a coincidence that an EMP shorted out all our vehicles as we were approaching the city?"

I shook my head. "Probably not. Goebbels probably picked us up. Have you ever heard of arcane power shorting out electronics like that?"

Nigel nodded. "It's actually a pretty simple thing to do. It was on our list of things I intended to cover with you."

"It didn't look simple. On that news feed it looked like a large flux of energy was pulled straight from the fissure."

Nigel nodded. "It takes a lot of power. It's simple to do, but also exhausting. My guess is that Hana had a battlemage who could do it or, given the fact that she's demonstrated an ability to cast across specializations, she drew extra power out of the fissure to do it herself so it wouldn't expend all her energy."

"That's something. At least we know that she's using the fissure for power."

"It's not much of something. Given the spread of the energies, it's just a matter of time before all the power she and her Axis mages need is all around us."

I nodded. "We might be able to use that as well. If you think about it, if we can cast here because we've reconditioned ourselves by going to the ethereal realms, it makes sense that we're drawing on power the same way she is."

"That's true. Then again, it doesn't give us any real advantage. She still has all the specializations at her disposal. All we have is battlemagery."

"Let's hope that apartment isn't a dead end. If you're right and the EMP wasn't a coincidence, if Hana did it to slow us down, then she knows we're coming. She'll be ready for us."

"Or she'll avoid us. She knows that we're not only battling her and her mages, but we're battling the clock. The longer she can stall and avoid us, the stronger she'll be. Goebbels might already have living mages in his back pocket. Without a visual feed of the fissure, she could be growing her resurrected army by the second."

The battlemages were gathered around us with their supplies in backpacks. I hoped they'd all packed water. With a walk this far they were going to get thirsty. I had a couple of bottles packed but I doubted it would be enough. Perhaps we'd find a tap somewhere between here and there.

"All right, everyone. Let's head out. We have to move fast, but we also need to preserve our energy. We're looking at an eight-hour hike, minimum."

We moved as a group down the highway. Since cars weren't working, we didn't have to worry about getting run over, and our broken-down convoy blocked the highway from the opposite direction.

The only positive thing we had going for us was pleasant weather. It wasn't raining. It was probably sixty degrees Fahrenheit. Don't ask what it was in Celsius. The whole kilometer business was already throwing me for a loop. Still, I was the lone American, and I could hardly expect the rest of them to abandon the metric system on my account.

Our small army was a fairly youthful bunch. I was hardly the oldest of them, though I was on the upper end compared to the rest. Most of them were in their twenties or thirties. About two-thirds of them were men, the rest women. All of them were well-trained and probably knew more skills than I did. My raw power was level five according to the assessment they'd done of my abilities when I first met the Entente mages. That meant I could access the highest amount of raw energy possible, per their classification system. According to Nigel, most of the battlemages were threes and fours. All that meant was that the spells I could cast had more juice than most. Since the others had a lifetime of training in the chambers on their résumé, they had a more diverse skill set.

Some skills I'd learned when I was younger, I hadn't used in years. I didn't even remember all of them. Taking nearly two decades off from casting hadn't seemed to weaken me, but it did leave me a little rusty. Thankfully, the fights we'd had lately and my training with Nigel had helped me get back into prime form —mage-wise, that is. I still had a lot of work to do to get into prime *physical* form. I'd been working out a lot over the last several months, but I still had a layer of blubber in my midsection. It wasn't as easy to shed pounds as it was in my twenties. At least with a fifty-kilometer walk ahead, I'd get in all my steps for the day. It was a shame I had forgotten my Fitbit. My steps wouldn't count. After a couple of hours walking, though, the blisters forming on my feet were more than enough evidence that I'd exceeded my ten-thousand-step goal.

CHAPTER TEN

We only made one pit stop, about four hours into the hike, at a gas station off the highway. The fellas could pee anywhere, but the ladies insisted we stop. It also gave us a chance to refill our water bottles. The station was closed, and we had to break in. My arcane missile that I cast to blast through the glass doors was probably overkill, but it worked.

The Gatorade was still cool. I grabbed one before the other battlemages raided the supply. Technically, we were stealing. Given the arcane apocalypse that was spreading, I figured we had a pass. I left what cash I had on the counter. It wasn't enough to cover everything everyone took, but it was something. I didn't have any euros. American dollars would have to do.

I also threw a couple of Snickers bars in my backpack, and I ate a third straight away. I probably should have grabbed protein bars instead, but have you ever tried those things? They might say chocolate and peanut butter on the wrapper, but that was just code for a flavor that more closely resembled butt and toe jam. At least what I imagined butt and toe jam might taste like. I didn't have a habit of sampling either.

The whole pit stop only took us about twenty minutes. It

would have taken less time if it weren't for the line of female battlemages that assembled at the restroom door. Even using the men's room in addition to the ladies', it took time, but twenty minutes wasn't bad, all things considered.

It was a good thing no one had to go number two. That could take twenty minutes per person. At least it took me that long. Then again, since our phones didn't work, it might have only taken five.

We hit the road again with a little more pep in our steps than before. My feet still hurt. So did my shins, my knees, and my lower back. At least the soreness wouldn't kick in for another day or so. I had to suck it up and keep going. If it got much worse, I could use my magic to heal myself. All mages could do low-level healing magic, though nothing especially potent. It worked well on scraped knees and paper cuts. It would probably handle the blisters on my feet, but it wouldn't do much for the soreness. I thought about healing my feet at the gas station, but at that point, the pain was reduced to numbness. I didn't want to go through the whole blister-forming process all over again. I'd heal my feet later. If I had a chance to do it after we arrived at our destination, I would, but chances were good we'd be busy. Blistered feet would be the least of my worries at that point.

The sun was already setting when we left the gas station. We were making progress slowly but surely. After it was dark we couldn't see much ahead of us. Under normal circumstances, a city like Berlin would be lit up and visible from miles out. Without any electricity flowing in the area, the city was as dark as the cloud-covered night sky that didn't offer us so much as a few stars, much less the moon, to brighten the road ahead.

Several bright violet-colored lights appeared on the horizon and moved toward us rapidly. I didn't have to question what it was. I grabbed Wand and quickly formed an arcane barrier as a barrage of blasts struck it.

"We're under attack!" I screamed.

The other mages didn't need any direction. They doubled up with one mage forming a shield and the other holding their wand, ready to shoot around it. I held my barrier steady and pressed forward as Nigel ducked behind my shield.

The light from our shields helped us see the army approaching. We had the advantage. There were maybe fifteen soldiers, all in SS uniforms, marching in our direction. They unleashed one blast after the next with shots fired in perfect unison. As we got closer, I saw their eyes. They were black. They continued moving toward us firing dark arcane missiles at us.

"Why aren't they shielding themselves?" I asked.

Nigel shook his head and reached around my shield to shoot a blast that struck one of the SS soldiers in the chest. The soldier collapsed and his body dissipated in a cloud of smoke.

"I'm not sure. I don't think they are acting of their own volition. All of them move in unison."

"Goebbels is controlling them?"

Nigel nodded. "I think so."

"They're shooting at us, but not defending themselves at all. I don't understand."

Nigel shook his head. "I don't know, either. But we're dropping them fast."

A circle of violet energy appeared over the top of the SS soldiers then dropped over them. We knocked down about half of them before they gated away.

I released my shield. "This makes no sense. What was Hana doing? Testing our strength? Would she sacrifice some of her soldiers to test us?"

Nigel shrugged. "These soldiers were either just a drop in the bucket, or it's worse than that."

"What could be worse than the notion that she has such a large army right now that sacrificing some of them wouldn't matter?"

"She raised them once, Thomas. What's to say she couldn't just raise them again?"

"Without bodies? Surely a body can only be used to resurrect someone once. She needs their remains."

Nigel shook his head. "Not if the fissure is changing our world. If the ethereal realm is pouring its energies here, it's not unlike the black mist that the fiends inhabited before. They don't need bodies to operate here."

I gulped. "And if she kills any of us…"

"Then she can probably raise us, too. Only then, those she raises will be under her thrall. Controlled by Hana through Goebbels."

I cleared my throat. "All of this begs the question, then. Even if we find Goebbels here, will killing him do any good at all?"

"Probably not. Even more, the most we can hope for if we fight against her soldiers is that we deplete their numbers temporarily. It's just a matter of time before they will come back again."

"If that theory is correct."

Nigel nodded. "Right. I hope I'm wrong. I don't think I am. If I am right, though, the only way to stop this will be to close the fissure. If we kill Hana it should close with her dead inside."

"That's not going to be easy to do. She isn't going to make herself easy to find and even if we did find her, she'd gate herself away before we could take her out."

"And since she has Goebbels, taking her by surprise is off the table as well. We need to find another way to close the fissure."

I huffed. "I say we stick to the plan. We go to that apartment and hope we can turn up some information that will help. All we know right now is that Hana was there personally. She was looking for *something*. Whatever it was, it's important to her."

"Even if we can figure out what she was looking for, chances are she already has it."

"If it's something important to her plan, then at least we'll know what we have to take from her."

"It could only be something so simple as information. You can't take information away, Thomas."

"We don't have any other moves. It could also be something more than that. Perhaps the apartment will prove a dead end. Maybe it won't. Still, we have to do something. Wandering through the streets and killing Axis mages who will come back again anyway isn't progress. At the very least, my instincts tell me that there's something in that apartment we can learn. Even if it's something small, it's still something. Right now we have nothing, and I'm not about to retreat and abandon hope while Nazis and Axis mages come back from the grave, make claims on governments, and unleash hell on Earth."

CHAPTER ELEVEN

We didn't encounter the rest of the small company of SS soldiers who attacked us again. They were in SS uniforms, but also had wands and could wield dark arcane magic. What we didn't know was if these soldiers were mages before or if they'd only gained their power and learned to wield dark magic in the afterlife. They had wands, but maybe that was a part of the welcome package everyone received when they descended into the realm of the dead. When Kat and I moved into our house, between our new neighbors and former friends, we ended up with two fruit baskets and nine casseroles. Nothing says "welcome to the neighborhood" like a casserole. I suppose nothing would ease the pangs of realizing you were dead better than getting a magic wand that allowed you to do things in death you could never do in life.

The funny thing about the casseroles was that at least three of those neighbors never reached out again, except to get their casserole dishes back. You'd think a better way to welcome someone to the neighborhood would be to invite them over, get to know each other, and maybe go out and do something together as families or couples. Making a casserole, I suppose, is a simpler way to say "we're not your enemies" without having to commit to the responsibility of friendship at the same time.

I don't remember anything about those casseroles, other than that most of them had a lot of cheese. Gotta love cheese. Usually. In St. Louis, we had a regional cheese called Provel. Like most things unique to St. Louis, it was an acquired taste. Less stringy when melted than most, more creamy like Velveeta, but a little sharper in flavor.

Given the lack of ability demonstrated by those SS mages, it might have been that they were still acquiring the taste for wielding magic outside the pure ethereal realm. Would they also get stronger as the ethereal energy changed the magical charge of Earth's atmosphere? Or were they destined to remain little more than arcane zombies, manipulated by Goebbels from a distance?

What about the ones we killed? If Nigel was right, they might come back again. They could come back, like each new manifestation of the McRib. Or, they could come back sleeker, a little stronger, perhaps with more personality, like the Volkswagen Beetle. An apropos analogy, given the history of that vehicle.

Never double dip. The rule applies to chips and salsa, and it also applies to people and the afterlife. I didn't know how they'd be different if Hana raised them again, but I suspected they'd be stronger. Perhaps that was the point. She wanted us to kill them. What doesn't kill you might make you stronger. What *does* kill you could make you damn near invincible when necromancy was involved.

The idea didn't fit well into a Kelly Clarkson chorus, but that didn't mean it wasn't true. One of the worst parts about a long walk like that, apart from the obvious aches and pains, was that it gave me too much time to ponder worst-case scenarios.

The only thing I could say with certainty was that those SS soldier mages weren't marching down the highway just to stretch their legs or to take a nice stroll at night. They were coming for us. Maybe they were testing us. Maybe Hana sent them to us to die, just so she could raise them again. Perhaps they were a warning shot. A threat to tell us we'd better not come any closer. If that was it, it didn't work.

We reached the outskirts of Berlin and used illumination magic on our wands to shine light all around. The closer we got to taller buildings, the more I was worried about arcane snipers.

Usually, if someone was about to blast me with arcane magic, my spidey senses went off a split second before. I felt it when they gathered their power. It worked differently here, though. I didn't feel anything when the SS soldiers attacked. I saw it and was able to intervene before their first barrage of arcane scuds took any of us out, but the only sense I had that worked was sight. In the city, with more buildings all around, we were more vulnerable. We had to stay alert and consider any possible location where some nasty dark mage might be hiding and waiting to fire.

If we had any familiarity with Berlin, it might have been easier. It's awfully hard to read a map and sort out where you're at and where you need to go when there's a potential threat lurking somewhere in the shadows.

Battlemages weren't even the biggest threat. If Hana could move her army with a single gate like that, she could do the same thing to us. She could use Goebbels to start screwing with our minds.

Being a sitting duck isn't all it's quacked up to be.

The further we went without encountering any more dark mages, the more anxious I got. If she wasn't attacking us yet, she must have a reason. She had a plan for us. Maybe she was just waiting until she had enough of a force at her disposal to guarantee no survivors. Her gates could do that already, though. What made me uneasy was the suspicion that she wanted us there, that she was using us, and that Goebbels might have been in our heads already working subtly and gradually to pull our strings with such gentle force that we didn't realize he was the puppet master and we were mere marionettes.

The closer we got to downtown, the more ominous things were. To be in a city like Berlin, at night, without *any* activity, any cars on the streets, no sounds pouring from the local pubs or anywhere else, was downright creepy.

We eventually found the apartment complex, and we divided up the group to search as much of the place as quickly as possible.

"You realize Hana and Goebbels probably know exactly what we're doing," I pointed out to Nigel.

He nodded. "Of course they do. It doesn't matter what move we make. They're going to know it. Any decisions we make from here on out will have to be made decisively and quickly. We'll have to make all our moves before Goebbels figures out what we're doing and Hana can respond."

I sighed as I headed up a narrow stairwell to the apartments where Hana and her SS compatriots had been sighted. "Until we have information we can use to make any decisions, it's hard to be decisive about anything."

"I told you before that I suspect you've inherited your grandfather's gift," Nigel insisted. "Trust your instincts. Despite your lack of training, compared to the others, you've managed to overcome foes as powerful or stronger than you multiple times. It's in no small part because you have a second sense about things. A hidden wisdom that shows you the path ahead. Don't ignore that."

I huffed. "Yeah, well, if Goebbels is in my head, how can I tell the difference?"

"Is it familiar? Listen to the voice you've trusted before. Goebbels might be a talented propagandist, and he might even be a decent impressionist, but he cannot perfectly mimic the voice of your conscience. Ground yourself with resolve, with your northern star, your family."

"Grounding oneself with a star is a confusing mix of metaphors."

"Not at all. The northern star used to be exactly how people navigated their path *on the ground*. Trust the light of your conscience that has always blazed bright within you. Follow the light that always leads you due north. Ignore impostors, false lights scattered in your mind intended to distract you."

I sighed. "It's awfully hard to do when the skies are overcast and I can't see any stars at all."

"Wait until the clouds part. That's why we're here. We're looking for something that will help us see through the haze."

We searched the apartments. If we had service, I'd have asked Nigel to send a DM letting our friendly tweeter know that her apartment was still closed and locked. It didn't matter. Hana's original specialization was portal magery. None of the doors were open, charred by arcane blasts, or damaged.

Until we got there, that was. We probably could have kicked the doors open, SWAT team style. I wasn't the only one with tired legs. Besides, a small zap to the doorjamb, one at the deadbolt, the other at the knob, was usually enough to bust a door open. The mechanics were similar to an arcane missile, but it involved a lot less power.

I allowed Nigel and the other battlemages to cast their arcane darts. Restraint was my weakness, and I tried not to cast indoors. It didn't usually go well.

It was a large apartment complex. We divided up into groups of ten. Most of the apartments were small, with only one or two bedrooms. I stuck with Nigel and eight other battlemages. The first apartment we searched turned up very little, apart from a cat that was none too pleased with our incursion.

There are few things more frightening than a pissed-off cat. I'm not too much of a man to admit it. I recoiled as it hissed at me, flashing its long fangs, arching its back with its tail poofed out like I imagined it might be after it took a ride in the dryer.

Nigel chuckled and grabbed the cat by the scruff on the neck to toss it in the bathroom.

"Afraid of a little pussy?" Nigel asked.

I cleared my throat. "In more ways than one. Especially a pussy with teeth."

Nigel smirked "Scaredy cat."

I shuddered. "Don't underestimate the fury of a pussy."

"I suppose I'll be searching the WC."

I nodded. "I'm not going in there with that thing."

Based on the decor of the place, this apartment was inhabited by an old woman. There were doilies everywhere. Under the lamp on the end table. Under a candy dish on the kitchen table. Under vases and statuettes on every surface and shelf. She collected elephant figurines, and I'd never seen so many miniature elephants in one place.

"I don't think we're going to find anything here," I admitted.

Nigel nodded. "We can leave five here to finish searching and move on to the next. I wouldn't discount what might be found in an old woman's apartment. If she was old enough to have lived through the Second World War, there might be things she inherited from her ancestors, like old records or perhaps old devices used by the Axis mages. Perhaps someone has the cremains of a deceased mage that Hana intended to raise. Since we don't know what Hana was looking for, we can't rule this place out entirely."

We were about to leave when we passed a bookshelf. My eyes were drawn to one of the titles. I would have missed it if the book wasn't at eye-level. I grabbed the book and handed it to Nigel. "Check this out."

"A copy of Heinrich Schwartz's *Arcane Theory.*"

I nodded and examined the other titles on the woman's shelf. "Check this out. These are all texts on different mystical traditions. There are three or four books here on druidry. Several more on what looks like witchcraft or wizardry. Some of these might be grimoires. I'm not really sure."

Nigel examined the shelves with me. "This woman must've been something of a scholar, a student of the various traditions. My guess is she wasn't a mage, but that doesn't mean she didn't dabble in arcane power."

"How could someone who isn't gifted in arcane power dabble in it?"

Nigel reached and grabbed what looked like the wordiest book on the shelf. He opened it. A few of the pages almost fell out. There were markings all over the pages and scribbles and notes in the margins.

"What is that?" I asked.

"A book on enchantments."

I raised an eyebrow as I read the title. *"Harnessing Mystical Powers Within Objects?"*

Nigel nodded. "Most enchanters don't belong to any particular tradition. They work with practitioners of various arts and combine their energies in unique ways to create objects of unusual power." He raised his voice and called, "Has anyone come across something that indicates the name of whoever lived in this place?"

One of the other battlemages grabbed what looked like an envelope from a drawer. "A stack of mail. It looks like this woman's name is Irene Dingel."

Nigel thought for a moment but shook his head. "That doesn't ring a bell."

"She may be a widow," I pointed out. "That means she might have a maiden name that you might recognize."

"Check the inside covers of the books," he suggested.

I grabbed the copy of *Arcane Theory* I'd spotted before. Nigel flipped back to the cover of the book on enchantment that he was already looking through.

Inside the cover of the book I examined, handwriting in an old script read, "To my daughter, Irene."

"Wolfgang Schwertfeger," Nigel finished with a sigh.

"Does that mean something to you?"

Nigel nodded. "Schwertfeger was an enchanter that worked with Nazis and the Axis mages. He was well known for creating enchanted blades that gave the men who wielded them unique abilities and skills."

"What kind of abilities?"

"Blades that could cut through anything with little effort. The metal was likely enchanted with arcane power. There were rumors that he'd experimented with using blades that wielded a gate mage's abilities. The problem was that a single blade could only form a portal to one place. Swing it in a circle and the idea was that a gate could form taking the person to wherever the original gate mage's spell originally intended."

I'd never heard of anything like that. "How could anyone possibly harness the power of a mage like that?" I asked.

"Enchanting is mostly harmless when it comes to working with other mystical energies. A witch's spell, for instance, can be harnessed easily by an object. To infuse an object, a sword, or anything else, with a mage's power requires a painful procedure. That's why Schwertfeger usually used swords. They had to pierce the flesh, enchant the blade by striking it through a mage's heart."

I gulped. "Let me guess. It kills the mage."

Nigel nodded. "Enchanting is strictly forbidden by mages for that reason. Schwertfeger participated in a variety of experiments alongside Mengele. Many of our brethren who were captured were tortured and subjected to their experiments."

I shuddered. "Horrific."

"Look at this." Nigel held the enchantment book open and pointed at a diagram. It looked like a human torso with a blade angled through the sternum into the heart. It detailed specifically which ribs the blade should be thrust between. "This is an extremely dangerous text."

"Do you think this is what Hana was looking for?"

Nigel shook his head. "She'd have taken it if she wanted it. I suspect that Irene likely had one of her father's blades. Something he'd enchanted during the Arcane Wars that held an ability she coveted."

"She's already a gate mage. That must not be it. I don't think she'd need a blade that could cut through anything."

Nigel looked thoughtful. "I agree. Whatever it was she took must've been unique. Perhaps it harnessed several different energies. Arcane power and something else."

"Hana wouldn't know about something like this. She must have learned about it from Goebbels."

"Without a doubt." Nigel nodded emphatically. "Or, perhaps from the Führer himself. If he's truly been resurrected as was reported. Something like this would have been top-secret. Very few of Hitler's men, even his most trusted, would likely know about it."

"There are a lot of notes in the margins of that book," I mused. "Perhaps there are other notes here we can use. We need to try and figure out what kind of enchantments Schwertfeger was working on."

Nigel looked grim. "There's no way to tell for certain that any of his experiments created whatever blade Hana was looking for. What she probably took from here. At the very least, it should give us a few ideas what she *might* be able to do with it. It could be key to sorting out exactly what her plans might be."

CHAPTER TWELVE

We tore the apartment apart. Irene's cat's meows from the bathroom were almost like howls. I tried to straighten up the doilies when we had to move them. We had no reason to believe that Irene had anything to do with putting one of her father's enchanted blades in Hana's hands. She'd studied her father's art, though. That much was clear from the books.

Only one person knew the truth. We didn't have any proof that Hana took a sword from the apartment. It was all conjecture. An educated guess. From the notes in the book, if Irene had one of her father's enchanted blades in the apartment, it could have been one of maybe twenty possible enchantments that Wolfgang theorized in the margins of his text. His notes weren't dated. I couldn't know if any of his "recipes" had been attempted, or when.

If our phones worked, maybe we could have tracked Irene down. Was she still in Berlin? Probably not. She'd likely evacuated with the rest. Still, her apartment was next door to the person who tweeted the picture of Hana and the SS soldiers. Perhaps we could have gotten Irene's number, or information about when she'd left and where she might have gone. Trying to find her was a lost cause. For all we knew, Irene had been in her apartment and Hana had taken her in addition to whatever enchanted swords she might have had hidden in her closet.

Nigel stepped up behind me, unzipped my backpack, and stuffed Irene's text on enchantment inside. "There's enough there that if we encounter whatever blade Hana might have stolen, it could be possible to disenchant it."

"How would we do that?"

"The notes indicate a precise balance between mystical energies necessary to sustain the enchantment," Nigel explained. "If we can add some extra energy to a blade, if we know what energies are at work, disenchanting the blade might be doable."

"I thought that enchanting a blade with arcane power required stabbing a mage in the heart."

Nigel made a face. "I said it would be doable. Not easy. It doesn't have to be one of *our* mages. If we can get our hands on that blade, it could be one of theirs."

I huffed. "Stealing a blade from Hana? It would be easier to kill her."

Nigel shrugged. "Possibly. If our odds of killing Hana are slim, a second move with equally slim odds doubles our chances."

I chuckled. "That's like saying that a glass isn't ninety-nine percent empty. It's one percent full."

"At least it isn't bone dry," he shot back.

The cat sounded like a demon screaming from a hole out of hell. "Feed the cat before we leave?"

Nigel smirked. "Good idea. I'll leave you to it."

I shuddered. "No way in hell!"

Nigel patted me on the shoulder. "The food is next to the bowl. You don't have to go into the bathroom with the cat. Just fill the bowl before we leave. You might want to top off the water bowl as well."

I decided to ignore this. "We aren't far from the fissure. Perhaps we should check it out. We know that Hana is likely monitoring our activities through Goebbels. She's stringing us along. The only way we might be able to draw her out is if she has to show up to stop us."

"Do you think there's a way we could possibly close the fissure? I don't know of any way to do it. Especially without any gate mages."

"We don't need to close it," I pointed out. "We have enough battlemages here that we could pool our power. Sort of like we did when we helped Jessie and Mary search the world to find the battlemages that Ichabod left abandoned on the glacier. We can cast a strong shield over the fissure. It won't close it, but if Hana is really trying to buy time to let more power escape the fissure, we can contain the energies."

Nigel considered. "It's risky. If energy continues pouring out of the fissure it will build up a lot of pressure under our shield. When we let it loose—"

"*If* we let it loose. We can hold the shield for a long time. I'm gambling on the idea that Hana might come to stop us. At the very least, she'll send some soldiers to distract us. If we have to turn and fight and divert energy from the shield, we might not be able to hold it, but we can rotate battlemages in and out of the group to keep up our strength. Whoever isn't casting to hold the barrier can defend the others."

Nigel nodded. "I like it. There's just one problem. If Goebbels is listening to us, they're hearing our plan even as we speak."

"Then we'd better hurry," I reasoned. "We may have to fight our way past some soldiers to get to the fissure. Hana won't show herself, and she certainly won't bring Goebbels, unless it's a last resort."

"The fight for the fissure. Sounds like something for the history books."

I nodded. "Absolutely. There's one thing about history books, though. They're written by the victors. Let's make history. This might be the best chance we have. If Hana shows, and she has the blade, we either kill her or take it. My preference is to kill her."

Nigel tilted his head. "Are you sure you can handle that? If it comes down to it, and you have the shot, are you ready to handle the temptation to the dark power that might accompany killing someone?"

"I downed Ichabod before," I reminded Nigel. "I did it to save my family. I didn't sense any dark energy at all. This is to save all of us. Besides, Hana is already dead. Putting her back in the grave isn't murder. It's putting her in her place—literally."

CHAPTER THIRTEEN

The cat was fed and watered, and we gathered the battlemages and left the apartment complex. We knew we were walking into a fight and that Hana most likely knew we were coming. The way I saw it, we were going to have to deal with whatever soldiers she'd raised, the undead or living mages recruited through Goebbels' propaganda. If we closed the fissure, they'd remain, so we might as well cull their numbers first. If we won and eliminated as many soldiers as we could, we could contain the fissure's energies and force Hana to come at us herself.

I checked the map before we left. I estimated it would be a twenty-minute march, give or take, to ground zero. Would she send all her soldiers to defend the fissure? I hoped so. Better to have our enemy in front of us, to know where they were, than to arrive too soon while more soldiers gathered to attack from behind, to force us to fight on two fronts.

We weren't going to win by out-strategizing Hana, not when Goebbels would know whatever we planned before we did it. The only way we'd win was through superior skill and determination. It would be a major test of our abilities. We were a group of battlemages that had a lot of training, but very little experience in real arcane battles. Conversely, many of the mages Hana was resurrecting were Axis mages who'd fought in the Arcane Wars during their previous life. Could advanced training overcome experience? Our battlemages were trained *specifically* to defeat the only enemy the Entente alliance had ever fought—the same dark Axis mages Hana was raising to fight against us. Granted, these Axis mages were different. We didn't know much about how their power had changed while they languished as spirits in the ethereal realm. We had no way to judge our odds of success. We didn't know the size of Hana's Axis army. All we had was one chance to take the fight to the enemy and force Hana's hand.

We divided our army into four groups so that if Hana sent her armies to fight at the fissure, we could come at them from several angles. It gave us the best chance to take them out. It also meant if Hana *did* have any troops in reserve, it would be harder for her to force our entire group into a trap against her army on two fronts unless she did the same and had enough soldiers to pin us down around the entire perimeter of the battlefield, a.k.a. the area around the fissure.

We gathered everyone together and selected four of the best battlemages to lead their respective contingencies. Nigel and I outlined positions on each side of the fissure. He would lead a group coming from the opposite side. The plan was to shoot a blast into the sky. When we did that, everyone would move in on the fissure at the same time. The enemy would see the blast. They'd know we were coming. They'd know our plan. So be it. They'd still have to defend against it.

The responsibility to signal everyone was on me. I was the only one whose army would have a clear view of the fissure and the enemy from afar.

We left the apartment complex and split up. I needed to give the other groups time to get into position, since they had a longer march to their spots. Nigel left first, and the other two groups left five minutes later. I left with my battlemages five minutes after that. Give or take, of course. No phones meant no clocks. Even Nigel, mister prim-and-proper, didn't have a wind-up watch.

When my army moved into place, we had a clear view of the fissure. We saw them, which meant they could see us. Hana wasn't there. The army we were facing in the middle consisted of about fifty Axis mages, some but not all wearing SS uniforms. That suggested some of them had been resurrected from the ethereal realm courtesy of Hana Sato's necromancy. The rest might have been raised, or they were living mages in the region recruited by Goebbels. Either way, we had a huge advantage. We outnumbered them and were coming at them from four different sides.

I retrieved Wand from my pocket and shot an arcane missile into the sky. Each battlemage shot a blast at the enemy. They raised their shields to deflect our strike. We expected as much. Before they could return fire, we raised our shields. We were going to have to fight this one up close, and I was going to get a chance to put my saber training to the test.

As we got closer, I looked ahead and to each side. The other mages weren't there yet. I had to trust they'd show up soon.

Our shields crashed against theirs. We dropped our shields and summoned sabers on our wands. The Axis bastards weren't ready for that, but a few of them launched cherry bombs in our direction. I wasn't sure how many of our mages were hit. There were a few screams behind me and the rest of us charged with a fury, cutting down the enemy's front line.

Where the hell were the other mages? They should have been there fighting from the other side.

Several blasts and screams in the distance suggested they were already locked in battles of their own. Hana knew our plan. She must have decided to split her army into groups as well, with one group defending the fissure and three more attacking the rest of our army in the streets surrounding ground zero.

That meant we were outnumbered two to one, even though their cherry bombs didn't take out as many of our mages as our initial strike against their frontline did. We had to beat them through skill.

Some of the enemy had black eyes. Some of them didn't. The black-eyed Axis mages were sloppy. If they were under Goebbels' control, that made sense. Especially if other dark-eyed mages were fighting our other armies. One mage manipulating the undead couldn't direct four different armies, consisting of dozens of mages, with much precision.

The living mages were more difficult to fight, but the advantage wasn't tilted in their favor as much as initially expected.

My fellow battlemages were impressive. A few of them fell, but they killed more than we lost. That didn't make it any easier, though. Losing a single mage was more than I wanted to sacrifice, but this was war. Casualties were inevitable.

In the chaos of the battle, it was hard to assess what was going on. All I could do was focus on the enemy straight ahead. Any distraction could kill. Only a few of the enemy had sabers—all of them living mages. I clashed with one, and my saber met his as he was attempting to charge me from the right. I pivoted and took a swipe at his leg then kicked him. Not enough to win, but it slowed him down. I brought my saber over my head and swung it down at him. He blocked it. I swung it around and went for a jab at his gut. He struck the side of my saber just in time, diverting my attack.

He knew what he was doing. I was still a novice, but I was fighting from what Nigel might have said was a healthy fear. The save-your-ass kind of fear that heightens your senses and enhances your resolve.

My opponent went on the offensive and swung at me from my right. I raised my saber just in time to stop his strike. He kicked at me, forcing me to jump back. Then he came back at me with a charge. I blocked him again, but I tripped over my own feet.

He twisted his body around and was about to strike me when a large blue blast caught him from behind. His saber disappeared and he dropped his wand. I looked past him and saw Nigel with his wand extended. He only had five other mages beside him. Had he really lost so many?

With the help of Nigel and the others, we made more progress and eliminated our enemies near the fissure.

Then two more groups of dark mages approached from either side. They were bloodied and battered. Five on one side. Eight on the other.

"Bloody hell!" Nigel exclaimed. "If it's the enemy coming in—"

"Then they defeated our battlemages. That's fifty men lost at least."

"And we lost most of ours."

I clenched my fist and grabbed my wand with my other one. "We might only have fifteen mages left when all is said and done."

"No time to mourn now. We still have to fight."

I nodded. "We stick to the plan. We still have enough to cast our shell over the fissure. We have to see it through, or their lives will have been lost for nothing."

We engaged the rest of the mages, splitting up into two groups as they closed in on us from either side. Nigel fought on the opposite side of the fissure from me.

The fight wasn't as vigorous as it had been when we first started. We had barely survived our battles. We were exhausted. We had to come through. Some of us had never been in battle before, but in less than thirty minutes, we were all battle seasoned. We all lost men who fought beside us.

I didn't want to lose another mage. I dug deep. I don't know where I found the energy from. Maybe it was from the pain I was suppressing after seeing so many of my brothers and sisters die. Perhaps my fear of failing had something to do with it. Whatever the case, something came over me and I fought like hell. I dropped dark mage after dark mage. As they fell, wisps of arcane energy flew from their bodies. The fissure sucked them in like a ball of dog hair into a vacuum. Nigel and the mages on his side of the fissure were fighting with just as much fury.

When all was said and done, our number was reduced to twelve. Not including myself.

A hundred mages. Down to twelve.

Nigel put his hand on my shoulder. "A Pyrrhic victory."

I shook my head. "I won't let that happen. We need to bottle up this dark energy. If Hana shows herself, I'll kill her myself."

CHAPTER FOURTEEN

The other twelve mages held hands and pooled their energy with Nigel at the end using his wand to cast a giant arcane barrier over the fissure. The fissure was probably half a football field long and twenty feet wide. Given the amount of dark energy flowing from the portal and the size of the fissure, it took a lot of power to contain it.

We tried it with eleven mages. It didn't work. It came down to either Nigel or me joining to cast the shield while the other faced Hana. I tried to tell Nigel that he was the one best equipped to deal with her if she showed, but he insisted that my experience facing her, not to mention facing Caedes, made me the man for the job. More than that, I *knew* Hana. Before she died. Before she came back. When she was just a girl, wide-eyed and innocent, Hana and I had trained together at our yearly convocations. There was more to confronting her than skill.

My magic, my unique signature, was part of what Caedes used to resurrect her. She couldn't kill me outright without compromising the magic that vivified her once-dead spirit.

On top of that, she knew that her son and I were close. What would Hans think if she killed his friend and mentor?

Hana told me the last time we met what she might do. She could bury me in an arcane prison, as I'd done to Caedes. She'd keep me alive but take me off the map.

If Nigel confronted her, there would be nothing to stop her from killing him. I had to be the one to do it.

The dark arcane power swelled under our blue arcane barrier. The combined colors made the barrier look like a long black light spanning the length of the fissure.

It was still dark outside, and the black light emanating from the arcane barrier gave the entire area a surreal appearance, highlighting some colors while not illuminating others. Flecks of something on my skin glowed under it. I had no idea what that might be, given all we'd gone through since we left St. Louis. Under other circumstances, with some heavy bass techno and a few mushrooms, it would have made for one hell of a rave.

This was no party. It was war. There was nothing celebratory about it. Knowing the potential of the power that swelled against the barrier, the arcane bomb that might go off if the battlemages couldn't hold it, the glow was ominous and terrifying.

I wasn't sure how long the battlemages could maintain the barrier. Our initial plan was to rotate mages in and out, but we didn't have enough left to do that.

I walked up and down the length of the fissure, watching in the distance to see if any other Axis mages showed up or if Hana might make an appearance from a distance.

A dark portal appeared ten feet in front of me, and Hana and Goebbels emerged.

I unleashed an arcane missile at her, but she waved her wand through the air, caught my missile, and deflected it. I'd never seen anything like that before, and I didn't have a clue how she pulled it off.

I grimaced and tightened my grip on my wand. "Don't bother, Tommy," she urged me.

"Give it up, Hana. It's over."

"Is it?" Hana smirked. "What is over, exactly?"

"Your plan to start another war. To take over the mage world and probably the rest of the world as well."

She laughed. "I don't *need* a full-fledged war to do that."

"Then why raise a bunch of freaking Nazis?"

Hana shrugged. "They share my vision."

"For racial 'purity' and world domination?"

"That *was* their vision a long time ago. You forget, Tommy, I've been dead a while. They've been dead a lot longer. There is much to love about this world. About being alive. There's also a lot of power in death, a connection to the wells that in some ways makes one feel more alive in death than in life. I'm here to give the world a gift."

"You're killing people!"

"I sent you a small group of my mages to slow you down. You're the ones who attacked us."

"Your mages slaughtered most of us!"

"Not as many as your mages killed. It doesn't matter, Tommy. What if there was no death?"

"You're talking crazy. Death is a part of life."

"It is. It doesn't need to be. What if there was less a barrier between the realm of the living and the dead, between the Earth and the ethereal realm, and more like an open border that people could cross with little sense of any difference between the two?"

I shook my head. "It's not possible. You'll never pull it off. You know as well as I do that there are beings in the ethereal realms that if they could move freely between our worlds would destroy everything we know."

"It would change things, I grant. But those who can harness the power of the ethereal realm, mages like us, could endure. Those who die, after a time in the wells, could one day emerge as mages. Reborn in power."

"You're talking about merging the realms?"

"Not completely. If I remember right, when we were kids, you played a lot of video games."

I shrugged. "So what? Most kids do."

"What happens when you die in a game? You re-spawn. You get another chance. I'm talking about giving everyone another chance. If the arcane laws of magic, rather than the laws of material physics, govern existence, there's no telling what could be possible."

I snorted. "I thought you were planning to turn the world over to your son."

Hana shook her head. "My son doesn't know what's best for him. I have to thank you, Tommy. You showed me that I was wrong. I was short-sighted. I don't need to take over this world like some kind of empress. I can change the world at a basic level. I can take the finality out of death!"

"You aren't who you used to be. Death, and returning through dark magic, warped your mind."

"I grew up, even in death. That's the difference, Tommy. You're still looking at the world from the perspective of a mortal. I am immortal."

"You can't possibly know that it would work," I insisted. "You came back from the grave, and it took a lot of power to do it. Caedes had to murder dozens of mages to do it. Even a fissure like this doesn't leave an open door for the dead to return. Someone like you has to draw them out again."

"And when my soldiers, raised by my power, channeling my energy, kill, I grow stronger. I gain the power to be the gate-keeper, to hold open the door, to draw out all of the dead!"

"I've seen the people you've raised. They're like zombies. They're under your control."

"Only because I hold them in my thrall. With Goebbels here, who also does what I wish, I can enthrall those I raise."

"You're talking about killing millions of people!"

Hana rolled her eyes. "I don't have to kill so many. Everyone will die eventually. Millions have died before. Billions, in fact. I only need to kill enough to gain the power to ensure that I can bring *everyone else* back to life again."

I shook my head. "And vulnerable to your control, your influence."

Hana laughed. "I can't control everyone at once."

"Maybe not. But you can leave them in some kind of stasis, like zombies, with no volition."

"A few more empaths, and I'll be able to do so much more!"

"You're not talking about saving the world. You're not even talking about taking over the world. You're trying to turn your-self into a god!"

Hana smirked. "A goddess, thank you very much."

I huffed. "You're insane. So what if death is no longer final? If the people you bring back no longer have free will, if they could at any moment become your puppets, that's not eternal life. It's everlasting slavery."

"Why don't you join me, Tommy? You could be divine at my side. You realize Caedes raised me using your magic. If we died together, and we returned, we'd share in our power. You could be the only one to hold me in check, even as I would have power over you when I pull you out of the realm of the dead."

I pressed my lips together. "Why don't I just use that power to control you now?"

"You haven't bathed for decades in ethereal power," she pointed out. "You don't know what's possible. If we die together, here and now, I will raise you again when you've come into your power."

I snorted. "I think I'll pass."

Hana approached me and raised her hand to my cheek. "You're still thinking like a man alive. You are thinking about the people you think you love. Do this for them. Be with me. Give your children the chance to live forever."

I narrowed my eyes. "This is crazy talk. If we died together, how would you ever come back to raise me anyway?"

Hana reached for a blade in a sheath at her side. "With this."

"Wolfgang's blade. It's enchanted."

Hana shook her head. "Not yet. It lacks one ingredient. With this blade, even in death, I'll be able to open a fissure from the other side. I'll enter the realm of the dead and blast it open. You have a choice, Tommy. Join me, or I'll do it myself. Even if this fissure closes, the power here is seeded in the earth. It won't just go away. You'll be stuck here while I break through the ethereal realm and make a new fissure, one far more powerful than this one, and sow the seeds of the new arcane world order in a place where some of the most powerful mages in the world now reside."

"You can't be talking about—"

"St. Louis. Thank you, Tommy, for bringing all the Entente mages together in one place. I will gather millions of the dead as I pass through the wells. I'll bring them with me and send every last mage in St. Louis to the ethereal realm so that I can raise them again. They will be my heralds, the first fruits of a new and better world. Will you join us, or languish here? You cannot portal out of here. There are no vehicles that can take you beyond this place. Before you could walk away to a place where a gate mage, my son perhaps, could get to you, I will be done. You will be too late."

I shook my head. "It won't work, Hana!"

Hana smiled and touched my cheek again. "I admire your resolve, Tommy. It doesn't matter how determined you might be. It's a simple fact. You have no way to stop me."

I jammed my wand into Hana's gut. "I wouldn't count on it."

I summoned my saber at the end of my wand, and it drove straight through Hana.

She gasped and formed a portal over herself and Goebbels. I turned and found her standing right above the arcane barrier.

She jammed her wand into the shield and channeled all the energy she had into it. The barrier flickered. I ran over to the battlemages and joined my hand to theirs. I added my power to theirs, but it wasn't enough.

The barrier faded. Hana plunged the enchanted sword into Goebbel's chest and pulled it out.

She drove the sword, still dripping with his blood, into her own heart, and both of them fell into the fissure.

CHAPTER FIFTEEN

The fissure shrank to nothing. Hana was dead. Sort of. She was coming back, and she had an enchanted blade that she took with her into the ethereal realm that she could use to come back to my hometown. The place where my family was. Where the other mages were. I could only hope that the mages left would figure out a way to slow her down, maybe even beat her, while Nigel and I and the other battlemages hoofed it out of Berlin.

Maybe it was just coming down from an adrenaline high from the battle. Perhaps it was a sense of hopelessness. We were battlemages. Killing shit was our forte, but we had nothing left to fight. What could we do other than walk until we could get to a place with a working phone? Only hope that so much shit hadn't blasted the fan in St. Louis by that point that we couldn't get ahold of Hans or Evander. We might not be able to reach them. If Hana set off the same arcane EMP over St. Louis that she did in Berlin, we'd be screwed unless we could reach a gate mage somewhere in America outside St. Louis. Even then, we'd end up back where we were before and have to hike our asses into the city as we did in Berlin.

All of that took the wind out of me. I sat on a piece of rubble. I took off my shoes and cast a stream of healing arcane magic on my bruised and blistered soles.

Everyone else looked every bit as dejected as I was. All we could do was hope that something might go wrong for Hana. Maybe her enchantment wouldn't work like she expected. Perhaps she'd stay dead. Not likely. You don't plunge a sword into your own heart, completing an enchantment like that, unless you're certain it is going to work.

Nigel walked over and put his hand on my back. "We should get moving."

I took a deep breath and released it. "I know. Every joint in my body aches. If Hana was telling us the truth, the bitch of it all is that it won't matter. We can bust our asses and find our way back to Missouri. Maybe it takes a day, maybe two or three, and we get there just in time to see a fissure worse than this one, something we can't seal, and a wave of unstoppable energy infecting the world."

"Are you still breathing?"

I nodded. "Yeah. So what?"

"Then there's hope. So long as you're breathing, you can fight."

"Hana invited me to die with her. Maybe if I wasn't breathing, it would be better. Then I could go with her and try to use whatever power I had to restrain her."

Nigel shook his head. "You don't mean that. It would change you. It would mean saying goodbye to your family, giving up on hope."

I rested my face in my hands. "I know. You're right. I'm just flipping out a little. A lot of people just died. I need a minute to get my shit together."

"I get it, mate. My mind is spinning too. I can't shake some of those images. Our brothers and sisters. What happened to them in the battle. I won't ever forget it. I'll probably need a bloody therapist to deal with it. This isn't the time to process all this shit.

The battle now isn't against Axis mages. Not here. It's a battle of our resolve against our fears."

I took a deep breath and stood. "You're right. I need to get back to my family. Whatever it takes."

Nigel patted me on the back. "Let's gather the others. The only thing we can do is keep moving forward."

I wasn't the only battlemage in our small group who was tired or troubled. I didn't know the battlemages who died very well. I couldn't even recall most of their names. The other mages had lived with them, though, grown up with them and trained with them in the Entente chambers. They had families, too. This wasn't my battle alone. It belonged to all of us. The only way we stood any chance to thwart Hana was to take the next step, the first of thousands, in our attempt to get home.

We headed back toward the street and saw an old woman standing on the sidewalk on the other side, staring at us. She was wearing a long floral-patterned dress and tennis shoes. Her white hair was pulled in a bun atop her head.

I crossed the street to her. "Are you all right, ma'am? You realize this whole area was evacuated. Do you need help?"

The woman smiled. Despite her age, she had perfect teeth, straight and white as printer paper. "You have my book."

I furrowed my brow. "Are you Irene Dingel?"

The woman nodded. "I do not need your help, *Liebchen*. You need mine. And I'd like my book back."

"My name is Thomas. Not Liebchen."

"It means sweetheart. I know who you are. I've been watching you."

I rubbed my forehead. "Watching me? How didn't I see you?"

Irene grabbed a ring on her left hand and twisted it. She disappeared.

I looked back at Nigel, but he only shrugged. I turned back and Irene was there, smiling at me as before. "How did you do that?"

"A simple enchantment, *Liebchen*. I know what the mage stole from me. I was listening when she told you what she intends to do."

"Do you know how we can stop her? I'm sorry. Maybe I should ask if you even want us to stop her."

"My papa was a man of his time. It is true, he did work with the Nazis, but that was a long time ago. I was just a girl. I didn't know any better and, in truth, neither did he. He wasn't an evil man. Like anyone who fights for a cause, he believed he was doing what was right."

I stared at Irene for a couple of seconds before I responded, "They were Nazis."

"*Ja*! They were. It's much easier to judge the decisions people made in the past when you already know how history has evaluated their actions. My father did not want to unleash evil on the world. I can say, with the same benefit of knowing history that you have, that he was wrong. Many of our people were wrong. In desperate times, good people who think they're doing the right thing often find themselves on the wrong side of history."

I scratched the back of my head. "I'm sorry. You're right. I'm not here to judge your father or anyone else. I just need to know if there's a way to stop Hana. She's the mage who stole your father's sword."

"Come with me."

I waved at Nigel and the others to follow. Irene stopped. "They can wait here."

"You can trust them."

"Maybe so. If you'd like my help, *Liebchen*, then you must come with me alone. What I have to show you, what I can teach you, is not knowledge that should be shared with others. Had I not heard you tell that mage what you did, refuse her offer, I wouldn't have shown myself to you. You saw through her plan, as tempting as what she proposed appeared."

I shrugged. "It wasn't *that* tempting."

"She told you that she had a vision that would strip death of its permanence. Certainly, a lesser man would find that a worthy endeavor."

"You don't think beating death is a good thing?"

Irene laughed. "Of course not, *Liebchen*. There is a reason the gods have limited our days."

I cleared my throat. "The gods?"

"I am a witch, *Liebchen*. I revere many gods."

I gulped. "What kind of witch?"

"I don't command an army of flying monkeys, if that's what you're worried about. I don't live in a house made of gumdrops, and I have no plans to throw you in my oven for dinner."

I grinned. "I know those are only stories."

"I honor nature. There are powers all around us. Spirits that inhabit all things."

"There is a lot of arcane energy in the air here. Hana said what the fissure released would remain."

Irene shook her head and laughed. "You mages are all alike."

"Not exactly," I protested. "We wouldn't have fought each other like that if we were the same."

"That's not what I mean. In the ways that matter, you are similar. You only acknowledge your own brand of power. Your arcane magic."

"I know there are other kinds of magic."

"Yes, but you imagine yours is the strongest, the profoundest of magics."

"I haven't really thought about it like that before."

"Still, like most mages, you don't think much at all about the force of nature, the power in all things, and you never consider it might be stronger than what you wield."

"Are you saying you have some kind of spell that can get me back home? That I can use to stop Hana?"

"You're asking the wrong questions. The spirits of a place, the spirits of nature, seek only to maintain order and balance. The power released here, that lingers in the air, does not belong here. It sets things out of balance. Even as death must exist to keep life itself in balance."

"I'm sorry. That sounds fascinating, really. But I don't understand. How will that help us?"

"You want to get home? Then we must fix this place. Appeal to the spirits to set things right again."

"You mean dispel the arcane magic?"

"In a way. Think of it more as a cleansing."

"If you can do this, why haven't you done it yet?"

"I intended to. It took some time to sort out exactly what was happening. Now that I know the nature of the energy that's infected the air, I know what to do. It may even be helpful to stop the mage and seal her up once and for all. To send her back to where she belongs."

"We can do all of that here?"

"Certainly not. But if we cleanse the area, perhaps your friends can bring you home."

"Can you teach me the magic to stop Hana when I get back?"

"I could, but it would take many years of practice. It's a good thing my father was an enchanter. I know a few of his tricks. I cannot teach you the spell, but I can enchant an object that may allow you to unleash the spell a single time. It will give you what's needed to silence this mage and set things right again. To restore the balance."

CHAPTER SIXTEEN

Irene invited Nigel and the other battlemages to wait in her apartment. She might not have trusted them with witchcraft, but she was hospitable. She had a large Tupperware container of chocolate chip cookies that she set out for our mages to enjoy. She'd baked them for her grandchildren just before the evacuation. How had we missed them when we searched the apartment? I don't know if I could have resisted sneaking one or two if I'd come across them. I grabbed a couple and followed Irene out of her door.

"Where are we going?" I asked.

Irene smirked. "I could tell you, but then I'd have to kill you."

"Seriously? You're taking me there."

"There are some secrets worth keeping. My apologies, *Liebchen*." Irene reached up and touched me right between my eyebrows, and everything went dark.

I gasped. "What the—"

"It's only temporary, dear. It's not that I don't trust you, but I can't risk Goebbels extracting the location of my sanctuary from your thoughts."

"He's dead. For now."

"For now. If you fail, however, there are things in my sanctuary I'd hate for Hana to get her hands on."

I nodded. "I understand."

"Rest your hand on my shoulder, *Liebchen*. I'll lead the way."

The elevator in Irene's apartment building didn't work. Keeping your hand on someone's shoulder while going down stairs isn't easy. Every landing, when we hit that last stair, I tried to take another step and ended up slamming my foot into the ground and nearly lost my balance. Holding on to an elderly woman to stay upright wasn't ideal, but she was stronger than she looked.

Irene led me outside, where it was so silent that the change in temperature and the breeze were the only reasons I could tell. She led me down several turns. A few times, she forgot to warn me that I had to step off a curb. Not a pleasant experience, but I managed to stay on my feet. I suspected she was leading me in circles to throw me off, but eventually, a door creaked and Irene led me into a narrow and damp stairwell.

I wasn't counting, but we must've descended a hundred stairs. I heard a key enter a lock and a click. The door squeaked open, and Irene grabbed my hand and led me inside.

The door slammed shut, and Irene touched me again between my eyes. My vision returned in a flash. The room was illuminated by several gas lamps hanging from the walls and a series of candles surrounding the perimeter of a giant pentagram painted on the floor.

Several shelves mounted to concrete walls were stacked with trinkets of various sizes and shapes. Some statuettes, more than a few elephants like the ones I'd seen in Irene's apartment. There were shields and swords. Necklaces of gold and silver with jeweled pendants dangled from nails on the edge of the shelves.

"Are all these items enchanted?"

"Most of them. Some are completely enchanted. Others are partial enchantments, like the sword Hana took before."

"Why did you have it in your apartment, anyway?"

Irene shook her head. "It was something I was working on for a client. I didn't realize it was Hana Sato all along."

"You knew it had to be enchanted by stabbing a mage, and you were willing to make it for a fee?"

"There are other ways to complete an enchantment like that," Irene explained. "A skilled witch, like myself, can extract a part of a mage's essence and use it instead. When I realized who she was, that she had Joseph Goebbels with her, it did not incline me to help. She took the blade, tried to kill me, and left."

"She tried and failed?"

Irene nodded. "Thanks to my ring. I disappeared and didn't reappear again until I showed myself to you."

I glanced down at the floor. "What's the significance of the pentagram?"

Irene cleared her throat. "Pentacle. The pentagram is the five-pointed star. The circle surrounding it makes it a pentacle. It sounds like a minor difference, but the circle is essential. It delineates connection."

"What kind of connection?"

"A little history, dear. The symbol made an appearance among early Christians. Each point represents one of the five wounds of Christ. In Taoism, it represented the five classical oriental elements of earth, water, wood, fire, and metal. In my practice, as a witch, it more commonly represents the classical Greek elements—fire, water, earth, air, and spirit."

"I suppose you'd say that's the right interpretation?"

Irene laughed. "All of them are right. The pentacle is about connection more than it is about differentiation. Each point of the star contributes to the rest. All are bound together. To simplify it all, no matter one's interpretation, the symbol conveys order and balance."

"So you don't turn people into newts?"

Irene laughed. "You've watched too many Monty Python

movies. That would be a violation of order. Much of what people think about witches is the opposite of what we truly do. We are not villainous, wart-faced hags. At least not most of us. A true witch, who honors the craft, is a guardian of the Earth, a partner with nature, and strives for balance in all things."

"Including life and death."

Irene nodded. "We do not command the elements. We work *with* the elements, including the spirits. We do not master the craft. We are mastered by it. I do not evoke the elements, the spirits, and the gods in order to use their power for my own ends. I evoke those things that I might be a servant to the elements, the spirits, and the gods."

"So how do we do this?"

"May I see your wand?"

I was a bit taken aback as I explained. "Asking a mage to touch his wand is sort of like asking someone if you can see his underwear."

"Would you prefer to show me your briefs?"

"Not at all!"

She chuckled and explained, "You can wield arcane power. The power in your wand is already sufficient to activate an enchantment. If I use your wand as I cast my spell, your wand will be vested with a new ability."

"What ability is that exactly?"

"To restore order. To set things right. To call the powers of the Earth together to cleanse the corruption that Hana has released from the ethereal world."

"This isn't going to screw up my wand, is it?"

Irene placed her hand on my arm reassuringly. "Of course not. If you strike one who was raised by necromancy, it will set things right. It will send them back to the realm of the dead where they belong."

"Is this going to change my wand forever?"

"It's hard to say, *Liebchen*. Perhaps the enchantment will burn out over time. Perhaps it won't."

I took a deep breath. I handed Irene my wand. "I'll do whatever I have to do to get back and save my family. To get back and stop Hana."

Irene smiled widely as she took Wand in both of her hands. She carried it almost like a baby into the middle of the pentacle.

Still holding my wand in both hands, Irene raised it over her head. "Oh, Great Goddess, Mother Earth, Mother of mercy and healing. Send the energy of Hygeia, to nourish this place from her sacred bow. Send the energy of Brigid and the healing waters that drain from her sacred well. Call upon Ceridwen, that she might pour out her cauldron upon the land. I evoke the Morrigan, the Phantom Queen, the governess of war, that she might disarm those who do the Earth harm and grant the mage who wields this wand the victory."

The lines on the pentacle glowed with a brilliant emerald light. It shot out over Irene from floor to ceiling, blasting through the roof above. The light gathered and settled on my wand.

Irene lowered the wand, turned to me, and smiled. "It is done. The enchantment within your wand will work in collaboration with your arcane power. Your present power will amplify the enchantment and fuel it like a battery."

I held out my hand and Irene placed my wand back in my palm. I closed my fingers around it. It did feel different. The energy was more stable, more mature.

When a mage first gets a wand, it develops something like a personality of its own. It reflects the personality of the mage to whom it belongs. Since I was sixteen when I received my wand, it was always a bit jumpy, eager, and energetic. It still behaved that way, sometimes spazzing out around beautiful females. What I felt when I took my wand in my hand after Irene enchanted it was a calm maturity. A restrained power, but a power stronger than before.

"What do we do now?" I asked.

"Well, child. The electronics here are still fried. You do not have a mage here who can take you away. If, however, your friends have been attempting to get to you, well, perhaps they'll find you."

It could work. If a gate mage and an empath came together and got into the city, they'd find us quickly. We were the only mages anywhere. At least so far as we knew. For that matter, we were the only humans apart from Irene I'd found in the city. Jessie would pick me up quickly. She knew me better than Mary. A half-second tapping into my thoughts and she'd know.

This plan depended on our mages back in St. Louis trying to come here. Would they? I had to believe they would, for two reasons. First, we hadn't checked in by phone. That would raise red flags. Second, if Hana had already re-opened a fissure in the city from within the ethereal realm, and things were starting to happen, they'd be desperate to find us to help in the fight. So far as they knew, there were a hundred of us. It would be shocking to learn that so many of our mages were dead. We were still the most seasoned and experienced mages in the alliance and, though nobody else knew it yet, my wand carried an enchantment that represented our only hope to stop Hana.

I twirled Wand in my hand. "Thank you, Irene. You're a lifesaver."

Irene smiled gently and nodded. "I know." She touched me between the eyes again and I went blind.

I sighed. "You just gave me the power of several pagan gods, and you can't let me walk out of here with my sight?"

"You saw many of my items. Some of them were made by my father. I've enchanted some myself. Perhaps there will come a time when we meet again, when I might have something that will help you. Until then, so long as you're vulnerable to Goebbels, the location of my sanctuary must remain a secret."

I nodded, resigned. "I understand. One question, though."

"What is that?" Irene asked.

"How can you be sure that Goebbels hasn't already probed your mind?"

"I'm a witch, *Liebchen*. I have more than a few tricks up my sleeve. My ring is not the only enchanted item I wear. I also have a pendant that protects me from certain arcane influences. Your portal mages cannot force their gates over me. Your empaths cannot read my mind."

I scratched my head. "Any chance I could get one of those?"

"If you wear one, *Liebchen*, it will also silence your powers."

"Only while I'm wearing it, though, right?"

"If it's touching your skin at all, it will work. I have one I can give you."

Irene stepped away from me and left me standing there, unable to see. I heard her steps and the metal of a chain sliding off a nail. Irene walked back to me and placed something soft in my hand. A velvet bag.

"Thank you, Irene."

"You need not be the one to wear it. A mage who holds this will be as vulnerable as any human. Their arcane magic will be neutralized so long as they touch it. It will also protect whoever wears it from portal mages or empaths."

Irene led me back out of her sanctuary, up the steep stairs, and outside. When we got back to her apartment, she returned my eyesight.

"Welcome back, Thomas."

I nodded at Nigel. "We have a way to stop Hana."

"I felt the change when the energy in the air faded. I knew it worked."

"Irene enchanted my wand. I can use it to heal another fissure if Hana opens one in St. Louis."

"Brilliant. Now, how are we going to get back home?"

I shook my head. "We wait. Unless our phones come back on, we have to hope our friends find us while we still have a chance."

"If you can close the fissure, won't that be enough?"

I sighed. "I hope so. But if Hana returns to the arcane well with that blade, she could just open one again. We'll have to get that blade from her. And if she's bringing back the dead, and they protect her, it won't be easy."

Nigel nodded. "No. But until a few moments ago, stopping her was impossible. Now, we have a chance."

CHAPTER SEVENTEEN

I didn't know how long it would take. I had to imagine that the mages back in St. Louis were trying to track us down since we hadn't checked in for quite some time. With only two reliable empaths who could travel with the gate mages to look for us, it wasn't like they could be on the job twenty-four-seven. They'd need to take breaks to eat, sleep, use the bathroom, whatever. If Hana had already busted out of the arcane realm and was in St. Louis, they probably had their hands full trying to protect the city and slow her down. I imagined it was an all-hands-on-deck situation.

The way I saw it, we had two choices. We could start hiking, which, if the gate mages found us, would be a lot of effort for nothing. Or we could bury our dead.

Sometimes doing the right thing isn't the most practical choice. Strategically, just in case our mages couldn't get to us or weren't looking, heading out of Berlin as soon as possible made sense. It didn't feel like the right thing to do, though. So many battlemages had followed me into battle and only a handful survived.

We didn't need shovels. We didn't need an excavator. We

would bury these people the same way I buried Caedes twenty years ago. They didn't require an arcane prison. They didn't need a vault or a pine box.

All I had to do was form a temporary arcane prison around the bodies, phase into an astral form, and pull them into the earth. We gathered all the dead together, and I formed the arcane prison around them.

Nigel stepped up to speak. I didn't know them as well as he did. "Today we bury our brothers and sisters, grateful for their sacrifice. We mourn their loss, but we celebrate their heroism. Let each of us vow to make their deaths count. The blood they shed waters the seeds of a victory, one that will ensure peace for all people. May their bravery inspire all of us to find a new strength, a greater resolve, and serve as our compass. May their spirits guide us from the ethereal plane, may they lend their power to us from the arcane wells, as a testimony to an enduring truth. We are stewards of a magnificent power. We are not lords of our magic. We are servants of the well, protectors of the Earth and all of mankind."

It was an inspiring speech, but the moment demanded silence rather than applause.

I didn't have his poetic words. "I just wanted to say thank you. I also want to promise that I will do everything I can to help all of us win this war and end the bloodshed."

Several other battlemages also stepped up. Some of them shared personal stories that spoke to the character and personalities of the fallen. A few of them said prayers and read scriptures or verses that accorded with their personal beliefs. Magery wasn't a religion. Mages among us represented nearly every major world religion, and a few practiced Wicca or druidry as spiritual paths that they believed enhanced their mastery of arcane power. I was more of an agnostic. I believed in a higher power, but I wasn't committed to the Episcopalian dogma I was taught as a child. I found value in all the spiritual paths that the different mages represented. Their words resonated with me, though they came from a variety of belief systems. The mages I knew didn't argue over their religious convictions. They respected one another and found common ground in a diverse spirituality. At the same time, they weren't shy about their views. They shared their perspectives without judging those who saw things through a different lens. Given the conflictual nature of most religions discussions I'd participated in before, it was refreshing. We followed a variety of paths, and we had our own journeys, but we were united in our conviction that power should serve those without it, not oppress. It separated us from our enemy, from the Axis belief that the strong were destined to rule over the weak.

I'd be lying if I didn't admit that a part of me envied the spiritual depth that some of the mages had. I tried to follow common sense morality, and it served me well most of the time. At times like this, though, I had to admit it must've been nice to have a cohesive framework, a worldview that helped them navigate the pain of loss.

I had the honor of taking our fallen mages' bodies into the earth. I phased into my astral form. It took a lot of focus to maintain an astral body, and even more to do something else at the same time. It wasn't easy. I didn't usually do it in a battle, for instance. Any adrenaline at all, and my body would snap right back into material form. Not a good thing when you're trying to carry a mass grave into the earth. I didn't plan on joining them for an eternal rest, so I took a deep breath and did my best to clear my mind before I pulled the entire prison down with me. Not six feet under. Probably twenty. Given the condition of the area, I didn't want their bodies to be disturbed if the German folk excavated and rebuilt the area.

It usually took a lot of energy to do something like that, but it was almost as if the ground opened up for us, responded to my will, and allowed me to bury our fallen without resistance.

Maybe it was the enchantment in Wand. Irene said it was a power from the earth. It made sense.

I returned to the surface and resumed my material form. The battlemages were all gathered in a circle, telling stories about the fallen and laughing about things some of them did. I was a bit of an outsider. I didn't grow up with them in the Entente chambers. Still, I listened to their stories and laughed with them. It made me feel like I was one of them. I suppose, in a way, I was. I didn't have as many stories to share, but I was there. These men and women fought at my side. We were the fortunate few who lived to fight again.

Nigel was telling a story that had everyone in stitches and tears when a blue portal formed right in the middle of the circle. When Hans and Jessie emerged, everyone cheered.

Jessie ran up to me and hugged me. "You don't need to explain. I can feel the emotion here. I can see their memories in my mind's eye."

Hans didn't have Jessie's advantage, but he connected the dots. He looked around at the relatively small group that remained and sighed.

"Let's get back home. We need your help."

"What is going on?" I asked. "Did Hana come back?"

"She ripped open the fissure again in Gregory Park," Jessie confirmed.

"She tore it wide open," Hans added. "It's not a small fissure like before. This thing spans half the park."

"What about the alliance? Is my family okay?"

"So far everyone is fine," she assured me. "Hana hasn't moved against us, but she's drawing an army up from the ethereal realm."

I rubbed my brow. "They don't have bodies. They don't need them."

"How can we stop them?" Hans asked.

I twirled Wand in my hand, and the green glow of Irene's

enchantment drew a circle of magic in the air as Wand spun. "I have a way to stop her."

"What is that?" Hans asked. "I've never seen anything like it."

"A witch did this," Jessie said. "A good witch."

I nodded. "The enchantment should set things right. That's how the witch explained it, anyway. I can send the dead back to where they belong. I can also close the fissure. First, though, Hana has an enchanted blade. Unless we get it from her and destroy it, she'll be able to come back over and over again, no matter how many times I take her down."

"She's growing her army larger by the second," Jessie warned us. "The longer we wait, the harder it will be to get to her."

I rested my hand on Hans' shoulder. "I'm really glad you found us when you did. Take us home, buddy."

CHAPTER EIGHTEEN

Hans' portal took us back to the alliance headquarters. Our mages needed to rest, and we needed to get the lay of the land, figure out what Hana was doing, and come up with an effective strategy.

I wanted to go home and see my family, but I had to see what Hana was doing first. If Hana stuck to the pattern she'd followed in Berlin, she'd flood the atmosphere with energy from the fissure that would neutralize most of our mages. We'd be left with nothing more than our dirty dozen of mages who'd barely survived the first conflict.

If she'd already resurrected all the mages we killed once, we'd stand no chance against them with barely ten percent of the force we had before. The fact that Hans was able to gate us back to the alliance and that Jessie's abilities were still working meant Hana hadn't gotten so far in her plan yet. I needed to get a sense of how much time we had to bring the rest of our force against her if we were going to stand a chance. The one advantage we did have, was that Hana thought we were stuck in Berlin, but I knew she wasn't wasting time. Her entire strategy was to leave us helpless halfway across the world while she built up an army we couldn't stop before we found a way home.

"There's a tall apartment complex just west of Gregory Park. You should be able to take us to the roof and we can look over the park, hopefully without her noticing our presence."

Hans nodded. "Does she have Goebbels with her?"

"I'm not sure. She probably raised him soon after she broke through the fissure. We should assume he is back."

"If he is, it won't take long before he senses your arrival. He'll know you made it back."

I nodded. "All the more reason why we need to know what we're facing as soon as possible. If she knows we're already here, though, it might not be a bad thing. It might force her to re-strategize."

Hans gated the two of us to the top of the apartment complex. We appeared behind a large air conditioning unit on the roof.

I stayed as low as I could and moved to the edge of the roof. It gave us a clear view of the park below.

Everything looked normal. No fissure. No Axis mages were lurking around. No Hana. No Goebbels.

"I thought they were here. A large fissure that spanned most of the park."

Hans scratched his head. "They *were* here. I don't understand."

I sighed. "Hana must've closed the fissure and portaled her army elsewhere. My guess is that she knew you brought us back and decided to relocate."

Hans grunted. "They aren't corporeal, right? They came back from the dead."

I nodded. "Our empaths won't be able to locate them. I'm not sure if they aren't corporeal. When Hana returned before, when Caedes brought her back, she had a body of a sort. It just wasn't *her* body. It was almost like the power she brought with her was so dense, so concentrated, that she *appeared* to have a body like anyone else."

Hans scratched his head. "Do you remember what Hana's father said when we went to see her family when she first started raising Axis mages? You asked him why Hana would want to raise her own body when she already had an ethereal one. Remember?"

I pressed my lips together. "He said something about distressed souls and how their traditions in ancestral reverence were meant to give untethered souls peace. By untethered he meant souls without a body. The body tethered Hana to this world, so she couldn't be appeased and released."

Hans nodded. "If you recall, Sato indicated that the other Axis mages were raised not through pure arcane energy, but in the flesh, because once they completed their mission and eliminated the allied mages it would put their souls at rest. Hana tethered them to the world so that even after they won, she'd still have them at her side."

"And he theorized that the same was true with respect to Hana's desire to give you the world," I mused. "Taking over the world, handing it over to you, would put her at peace. She still wanted that, but she tethered herself to her body so that wouldn't be an issue."

Hans pinched his chin. "Now that she doesn't have a body, she is vulnerable."

I huffed. "Sure, if you become the emperor of the world, maybe her spirit will be released and forced back into the ethereal plane for good."

"I'm just saying, maybe there's more to it than that. It was just a guess that she wanted to take over the world to give it to me. That's a pretty big stretch, don't you think? I don't know my mother well, but what if it was simpler than that? That's why she was afraid before and raised her body because she was afraid that if I was happy and well, she couldn't hold on."

I paced across the roof of the apartment complex. "She

wanted you to join her for sure. When you refused, when you opposed her, that didn't change her ambitions."

"She abducted me to take me away from you. You've given me a chance to be a part of a family. I know your family isn't mine. I'm not trying to push myself in or anything."

I shook my head. "You are a part of my family now, Hans. You aren't intruding. You're like a fourth son to me."

"What if that's what she was afraid of? That I'd find peace, a happy life, and my well-being would no longer keep her spirit tethered to the world? That might be why she resurrected her body. Why she worked so hard to lure you to Berlin in hopes you'd fail. It's just an idea. If we can't get to her through battle, if her forces are too strong, and we can't get that sword away from her, perhaps there's another way to appease her spirit and send her back."

I bit my thumbnail. It was a bad habit that I often turned to when I was in deep thought. "There's one thing Kat wants more than anything else. It's what I want for my boys more than anything else. It's what every parent wants. Sure, we want our children to be happy and belong. First, though, we want them to be *safe*."

"Why else would she bring the war to St. Louis? The same place where you and your family live? She could resurrect her mages anywhere. She could recruit an army from dozens of other mage-populated cities around the world. Deep down, so long as I'm not safe, she knows she can't be at peace. It's a bit of a catch twenty-two. She's denying herself peace. She wants me to be in danger's path, so she can pursue her aspirations."

I shook my head. "That still doesn't track. She could have gated herself away from Berlin. She didn't have to kill and resurrect herself again. She did that on purpose. She said she was going to defeat death itself, to blur the boundary between life and death, so that anyone who died could come back again."

Hans gulped. "She didn't come here just to keep me in

danger's path, to stay on Earth as a spirit. She came here because if I won't join her, she wants to take me with her back to the ethereal realm. She wants me to die so I can rise with her in this new world where death isn't permanent."

"If that's true, she still has to finish her job and blast open the ethereal realm. She has to spread the energy throughout the world that she first did in Berlin."

"Once she does that, she'll kill me. So I can join her as she is."

"If that's the case, there must be another fissure. She must have a plan to seed the rest of the world with arcane energies. The question, then, is how is she doing it and where is the other fissure?"

"I don't know. You're right, though. Bringing you back so soon interrupted her Plan A. She must have a Plan B in the works. If we don't figure it out soon, it doesn't matter what her plans are for me."

CHAPTER NINETEEN

Hans took us back to the alliance headquarters. The mages we brought back from Berlin were mostly sleeping, and nearly everyone else was having lunch. Nigel was in the cafeteria, picking at a turkey leg.

We explained the situation. It wasn't good news that Hana wasn't where we thought she was. She hadn't given up her plans. She'd closed the fissure for a reason, probably because we got back from Berlin faster than she anticipated. It would have been better if we knew where she was and if we had a clear idea of what her plans were. Instead, all we had were theories and ideas. What if I could pacify her spirit without killing her outright? What if it was so simple as making sure Hans was safe? That might be good news, but we couldn't verify that idea, much less afford to experiment with attempts to untether her spirit from the world. Perhaps she had new tethers, new goals that would be unresolved even if we resolved whatever angst held her in the earthly plane when Caedes first brought her back from the dead.

Nigel took a bite of his turkey leg. "All we know is she has to be stopped. Your enchanted wand can do it. Getting the sword away from her is the priority. All of this raises a question, though.

From what we read in Irene's enchantment book, if a gate mage enchanted an object the way she did, it would basically be a single destination gate. Whatever gate she had in mind when she stabbed herself, the sword will only open a portal there."

"That's helpful only in terms of predicting where she will come back herself if we kill her, or if she kills herself again," I pointed out. "Any dark magic can create a fissure. She's already shown the ability to use necromancy to resurrect the dead."

Nigel nodded. "Still, she had to kill herself over the fissure to take the blade with her. If you could kill her with your wand, do we really know if the sword can make the trip? She doesn't have a regular body. It's only a projection of her spirit, of her mind, that *appears* real because of the strength of her power. That sword, though, was certainly a physical object."

"Maybe she's changed it into an ethereal item."

Nigel shook his head. "The whole point of an enchantment is to be able to put something that's rooted in non-material mystical energies *into* a physical device."

I pressed my lips together. "She'll likely stay near a fissure if she thinks we're going to attack."

"Maybe not," Hans suggested. "She only needs to know where a fissure is. If she comes under attack, unless you can be certain you can strike her and kill her instantly, all she'd need is enough wherewithal to cast a single portal, and she could drop herself back into a fissure."

I scratched the back of my head. "I guess all we can do is have our gate mages and empaths comb the area and see if they can come up with anything."

"Go see your family," Nigel ordered gently. "There's nothing you can do here. Get your rest. It's only a matter of time before she turns up. You need to be ready when that happens."

"I'll come with you," Hans offered. "There are plenty of gate mages here. Since we don't know what Hana's plans are, it's probably a good idea to stick together."

"Thank you," I said. "If Hana comes after me, or my family, I could certainly use your help to keep them safe. Not to mention, like I told you before, you're a part of the family now."

Hans smiled. "I appreciate that."

"First things first," I added. "We're bringing home some food."

"It's only the lunch hour. Plenty of time before dinner."

I chuckled. "Exactly. Best bring home something good before Kat throws something frozen in the oven."

"Those lasagnas aren't half bad. Just as good, I think, as most homemade lasagnas."

I nodded. "They are great. Not when you have them every week."

Hans and I approached the cafeteria counter. "Thomas!" Louisa smiled at me widely. She was an older lady, a domestic mage who'd prepared meals for the Entente mages ever since she was a girl. I wasn't sure how old she was exactly. She could have been my grandmother and, since I was over forty, that had to put her at eighty or above. She didn't show it, and she wasn't slowing down. Her domestic magery allowed her to whip up a gourmet four-course meal in a matter of minutes.

"Hello, Louisa. I'd like to bring a meal home to surprise the wife. Any suggestions?"

"What do you like?" Louisa had an accent suitable for the royal family.

I chuckled. "So far you haven't made me anything I didn't like. If you can sneak vegetables into something so that the kids will eat it, and so my oldest won't gate them off his plate and into the yard, that would be good."

Louisa snapped her fingers. "Shepherd's pie it is! I'll get started straight away."

I smiled. "Thank you, Louisa."

I didn't know how she pulled it off. Domestic mages didn't need conventional ovens. They had magic that could cook a meal in half the time. Despite the expedited process, nothing ever came out dry. The meats were juicy. The vegetables were always tender, but not too soft. Everything was always like the littlest bear's porridge—just right.

I was fortunate to grow up with a domestic mage. My mother was a fantastic cook. Kat tried her best, but she didn't have the advantage of arcane cooking in her arsenal. Combined with the hecticness of managing three children, a photography business of her own, and filling in at AAA Tool Rental, frozen and boxed meals were typical. Fast food and pizza delivery frequented our dinner table more often than any of us would like, and a steaming shepherd's pie was going to be a treat for everyone. I still hadn't eaten since I'd stuffed my face with garbage food at the abandoned convenience store in Germany. My tummy was growling like an ethereal fiend.

When Louisa was done, the smell of the food turned my stomach's growl into a roar. Thankfully, with Hans taking us back, I wouldn't have to wait long to dig in. Sure, it was early for dinner, but I couldn't have cared less.

Hans formed the portal, connecting the opposite end to my living room. We appeared in an empty room.

"Where is Kat?" I wondered out loud.

"Probably working," Hans guessed. "The kids still at school?"

I glanced at the clock on the microwave in our kitchen. "We have a few hours."

"Are we seriously going to wait to eat that thing?"

"Small portions. There has to be enough for Kat and the boys."

Hans smiled. "I always have small portions."

"Your portions would be small if you were a Tyrannosaurus rex. I wouldn't put it past you to eat this whole pie."

"How much you want to bet I could?"

"None! Because no bet is worth letting you have the whole thing. I'm starving! And this is for the family."

Hans chuckled. "Well, a small plate for each of us can't hurt. Might as well stuff our faces while we wait."

CHAPTER TWENTY

It took every ounce of willpower I had—which wasn't a lot—to stop at one plate full. It was the perfect blend of meat, potatoes, vegetables, and gravy. There were probably a variety of spices in there, too, but I didn't have a clue what they were. I didn't care. It was a whole lot of yum.

The kitchen was a mess. It was impressive how many dishes Kat managed to fit into the sink. They were piled up so high that if I pulled a plate out I was afraid they'd all come tumbling down like a Jenga tower.

I opened the dishwasher, and of course it was full. Hans and I tag-teamed it. We put away the clean dishes from the washer, then he gathered the stray dishes, half-filled cups of juice, and plates with dried food that were left all around the counters and brought them over as I carefully rinsed the dishes in the sink and loaded the dishwasher.

I would have allowed Hans to load it, but dishwashers have a learning curve. I had my own way to load it, and I knew how to get as many dishes as possible into the thing. We were going to need as much dishwasher space as possible. It looked like Kat hadn't done dishes since I'd left for Berlin.

Not that I blamed her, and I wasn't angry about it. While we had a little time, I figured it would be a nice surprise. Sure, I was just back from the war, and I'd seen some horrific things, but Kat was left handling all the kids alone. One parent and three kids? It's enough to push almost anyone to the edge of their limits.

Doing the dishes this time was almost therapeutic. Not usually. Most of the time I hated it. What happened in Berlin was still sinking in. Flashes of my fellow battlemages falling, struck in the chest with dark magic, popped in and out of my mind. I'd been in a few battles before, but nothing I'd ever seen in the past compared to the most recent fight.

I was doing the dishes to help Kat. I was also doing it because a part of me knew if I sat with my thoughts I couldn't help but think about that damned battle. I wasn't a soldier. I wasn't trained and prepared to deal with the things I'd seen. I had a cousin who served as a Marine in Iraq. He *was* trained and prepared the best way anyone could be, and he'd never been the same since. He was still a good guy. He had kids who were a few years older than mine, also all boys. A dark cloud surrounded him, though. There was something unmistakable in his eyes whenever I saw him. It was a pain, a wound, that his best smile couldn't hide. He never talked about the war. Not with me, at least. He only talked to other soldiers. They were the only ones who could understand what he'd been through and, just as importantly, what he was going through still.

He and his wife had bought several acres outside the city. They didn't raise cattle or grow crops. It was just grass to mow. Enough that he could spend an hour or two every day cutting, then he could start over again. After a few difficult winters, he took up rebuilding old cars and woodworking. He didn't have much passion for either hobby. It was just something to do, something to occupy at least a small portion of his mind.

I never understood what he was going through, but I was starting to. I couldn't talk to Kat or Hans about what happened in

Berlin. I could talk to Nigel. He was there. I couldn't *not* talk to Jessie, because she'd hear my thoughts whether or not I spoke. If she did, I hoped she'd ignore it. Maybe she'd know not to bring it up, not to say anything. If she knew and understood what I was going through, she'd also know that it wasn't something I could talk about. Or maybe she'd sense nothing, because I felt nothing. That was the worst part. The numbness. I should have felt more. It was the *not* feeling that terrified me the most, that made me think something was wrong. Maybe that would change someday. A part of me knew that I'd have to go through something like that again to stop Hana, and I couldn't allow myself to feel too much because I couldn't let myself fall apart. I had to stay strong, soldier on, and stop Hana once and for all.

What was more disturbing than any of that was that I was looking forward to it. I'd had a taste of battle and something deep inside me liked it, even as I hated it. I was scared of fighting again but missed it. How fucked up, right? That's not something I could talk about with Kat or anyone who wasn't there.

So I scrubbed the hell out of the dishes. When the dishwasher was full, I washed the rest by hand. Hans had a towel and dried the dishes and put them away.

When the dishes were done, I wiped down the counters. When the counters were clean, I vacuumed. It sucked. Because it was vacuuming. My jokes are awesome. After that, I dusted the shelves and the cabinets. I picked up all the kids' toys in their rooms and put them away, though I didn't sort them like Kat would have done. What was the point? Action figures in one box. Dinosaurs in another. Matchbox and Hot Wheel cars had a tub of their own. If I put everything back where it belonged, it would take the kids less than five minutes to dump it all out and return their rooms to the usual state of chaos.

I arranged their stuffies on their beds. Elijah lost interest in stuffies a few years back and had moved on to collecting Pokémon cards. My two youngest, Ezra and Elliot, had quite the collection. I couldn't call them stuffed *animals*. When I was a kid, I had teddy bears and Pound Puppies. Kids these days had stuffies that resembled their favorite computer-generated cartoon characters, and some of them were rather odd. They didn't resemble anything from the real world, certainly not animals. Still, the boys loved them. Anything that made them feel more comfortable in their own beds meant that Kat got to spend more nights in ours next to me.

Hans stopped helping after we finished the dishes and parked himself in front of the television to binge a show on one of the half-dozen streaming services I'd signed up for when we cut the cord from cable. For some reason, multiple small charges of fourteen bucks, give or take, seemed more economical than the single overpriced cable bill even though, in reality, it was probably a wash.

I finally heard the familiar roar of the garage door opening. Kat was home. I hurried back to the door off the kitchen that led to the garage and waited. Elijah came through first and ran up to me to wrap his arms around me. Before long, I had three kids hanging off me. For a moment, I was okay. I was grounded. I was at peace. I held my boys tight. I knew it wouldn't last. I still had a lot to do, but hugging my kids was exactly what I needed to find my strength again.

Kat stood at the door smiling widely. "Welcome home. Is it done?"

I shook my head. "Not even close."

"You weren't answering my texts. I was getting worried."

"It's a long story. Berlin was basically wiped out. No cell service. No electricity."

"I knew you'd make it back. You always do."

"A lot of good mages didn't make it. I can't stay long. I did bring home dinner."

I stood and Kat kissed me on the cheek. "Then we'll have dinner."

"Notice anything different?"

Kat laughed. "You cleaned."

I smiled with pride. "I certainly did. Hans helped with the dishes."

Kat was still chuckling. "Do you know how many times you've been gone at work all day and I spent the day cleaning? You do it once and need an 'atta boy.'"

I grinned. "I'm a man. I need treats. Positive reinforcement."

"How soon do you have to leave?" Kat smirked and tilted her head.

"I'm not sure. The other mages are doing some recon, trying to track Hana down. Until then, I'm supposed to get some rest."

Kat leaned in and whispered in my ear. "Let's hope you have long enough that we can put the kids to sleep. I can give you your reward *before* you get your rest."

I smiled widely. "I like rewards!"

Kat winked at me. "That's a good boy."

I chuckled. "I was hoping you'd call me a naughty boy."

Hans heard us and groaned.

Kat and I both laughed. "Mind your own business, young man!"

CHAPTER TWENTY-ONE

The boys devoured the shepherd's pie. Elijah had three servings and still complained he was hungry. I swear, there wasn't enough food in the house to ever fill that boy up. He ate more than I did and didn't have an ounce of fat on his bones. Everything he ate went into making him taller. Everything I ate made me wider. That kid was going to be taller than me before he hit sixteen.

The dishwasher was full of clean dishes from the load I had done before, so I started unloading it. Elijah set his plate next to the sink.

"Daddy, when do I get to train with Evander again?"

"I don't know, son. There's a lot going on now. Hopefully soon."

"Good! Because there's so much more power now."

I stopped what I was doing and looked at him. "More power? What do you mean?"

"More power. It's all over the place. It feels different."

"Different like how?" I asked.

"It feels dirty. But some man keeps telling me to use it."

My blood ran cold. He was talking about Goebbels. "Don't listen to him. Whatever you do, don't access that power."

"What is he talking about, Tom?" Kat asked.

I clenched my fists. "It's Goebbels. Hana closed a fissure she made at the park when I got back. I don't know if she can raise more dead mages for her army. During the Arcane Wars, Goebbels used his abilities to spread a brand of propaganda to recruit other mages to the Axis cause. He must be doing the same here."

Hans walked over to us. "It's more than that. Elijah, you said you sense other power? Something different?"

Elijah nodded. "I was hoping Evander would teach me how to use it. I don't trust that man who is talking to me."

"You shouldn't trust him," I urged.

Hans grabbed my arm. "A minute?"

I stepped aside and followed Hans back into the living room. Kat joined us.

"I didn't want to scare your son. Before a gate mage gets his wand, the energies we pick up can be overwhelming. I think it's because any energy that comes from the arcane wells is pure and raw, sort of like the raw magic we channel to form gates."

"If you set down your wand, can you sense it, too?"

Hans shook his head. "Once a gate mage is attuned to his wand, all the energies we access come to us through the wand. It gives us better focus, more control. It's how I can gate across almost any distance now. There's no going back. If Elijah is sensing dark magic, then Hana is leaking it out into the world somehow."

"Why isn't it neutralizing everyone's power like it did in Berlin?"

"If Goebbels is recruiting the local American mages, all those who haven't joined our alliance, neutralizing their power would be counterproductive. It took a large flow of energy from the fissure in Berlin to do it. What if she's releasing small amounts of energy through pinholes rather than fissures? Enough power that she and her undead mages can use it to gain an advantage, but not so much to silence our power. Not yet, anyway."

I rubbed my brow. "I don't understand. Why not leave the fissure, draw a shit ton of power through it, and neutralize us? Why would she need to recruit more mages if most of our mages couldn't fight?"

Hans sighed. "I don't know."

"We should tell Nigel. He might know more about what she could be doing."

Hans shook his head. "Stay here with your family. I'll go tell Nigel. Enjoy your family. Keep an eye on your son. These pinholes might release just enough dark energy to tempt mages. It's probably how Goebbels is luring mages to his cause. All he has to do is convince them to use that magic once and they'll be hooked. Trust me, as someone who has dabbled in dark magic before, it's not easy to shake off."

I shook my head. "It took your grandfather's sacrifice to free you from its hold on you."

"Maybe that's protecting the alliance now. The sacrifice of the mages who fell in the battle."

I took a deep breath. "It's a nice thought, but I don't know if it works that way. My guess is that if Goebbels is recruiting mages, he isn't trying to reach the alliance. They're trained to resist his propaganda. It's a part of the curriculum they used to teach in the Entente chambers. Hana doesn't want us to know what she's up to. If he tried to recruit our mages, we'd find out."

Hans nodded. "What Hana didn't consider was that your son might hear Goebbels. Hana doesn't know he has manifested."

I shook my head. "Or she does know, and that's her plan. To try and recruit my son to the dark powers. She can't kill me. That doesn't mean she can't hurt me. What better way to try and break my spirit, to convince me to stop fighting and embrace her plan, than to bend my son to her side?"

"We should call your mother," Kat put in. "Perhaps she can

ward our house. Would that stop Goebbels from reaching Elijah?"

I nodded. "It should work."

Hans pulled out his wand and formed a portal. "I'll go report what we've learned to Nigel. Stay here and keep your family safe. I'll be back when we have a theory or, better, a plan."

I stopped him. "I hate to think it, but if Goebbels is messing with American mages, my parents might be compromised. Send Louisa back here. She's part of the Entente alliance. She can ward the house."

Hans slapped me on the back. "I can do that. I'll send her through a portal soon. I'll come back when I have news."

CHAPTER TWENTY-TWO

For an elderly lady, Louisa moved fast. She was probably a decade and a half older than my mother. As a domestic mage, she was more skilled, and that's saying something because my mother was no slouch. The reclusiveness of the Entente mages over the last half century made them out of touch with a lot of the features of the modern world—like the Internet—but the almost universal focus on refining their magecraft meant that they knew how to maximize their natural talents.

Take the battlemages, for example. Most of them didn't have the raw power that I did, but what they did have they used more efficiently. If I was a chainsaw, they were surgical scalpels. My battlemagery tended to leave behind a lot of peripheral destruction, while they accomplished exactly what they intended nearly every time.

If I harnessed my strength with their precision, the sky could be the limit. Until Hana was out of the picture and we weren't on the brink of the Arcane Wars, Part Deux, it wasn't possible. At least I had my Jedi-mage lightsaber now. It had already proved useful in the battle for Berlin. What I needed wasn't more arcane refinement, but better sword-fighting skills. Where's a samurai warrior when you need one?

Louisa took a whole ten minutes, give or take, to ward the house. So long as Elijah remained inside, Goebbels couldn't reach him.

With the house warded, Louisa baked an apple pie and some kind of English dessert she called Spotted Dick.

Elijah couldn't stop laughing about it, but I was trying my best to keep the jokes to a minimum. There weren't a lot of good jokes I could think of that were appropriate in the company of children.

I had to admit, Spotted Dick was delicious. Normally I'd think something like that needed a cream, maybe some antibiotics. Louisa did prepare a cream that she poured over it, which begged for another half-dozen jokes that I had to keep to myself. It was a custard, and it was freaking amazing.

I kissed the kids goodnight and Kat took them back to bed. They still liked to have one of us in the room when they fell asleep. If any of them woke up at night, they usually ended up in bed with us. The chance that all three would sleep through the night was roughly fifty-fifty.

Louisa cleaned up the kitchen while I waited for Kat to emerge from the boys' rooms. Elijah usually went to sleep fine on his own—but not always. Kat usually started the bedtime routine with Ezra and Elliot. They shared a room and a bunk bed. Given all that was happening, Elijah needed a little extra company to fall asleep. I sat next to his bed until he passed out, which didn't take long after all he ate.

While I waited for Kat, I flipped on the local news. Without cable, I relied on the antenna to pick up local stations. They were still channeling the national broadcast. They didn't have a bird's-eye view of Berlin since the EMP had neutralized everything. They did have satellite imagery and a lot of pundits who had opinions. Was it terrorism? There were rumors of a leader, claiming to be the reincarnation of Hitler, demanding control of the government. Of course, the folks on television didn't believe he was who he said he was.

I'd almost forgotten about him. I'd assumed he was one of many who Hana raised from the dead. Whether he was actually Hitler was hard to say, but whatever the case, it dawned on me that if I could defeat Hana and seal whatever pinhole leaks of dark arcane magic she'd made, it wasn't going to be the end. There'd still be Axis mages and resurrected tyrants to deal with.

Louisa sat next to me as we watched the broadcast. I rested my elbows on my knees and my chin in my hands as I watched. "Do you think it's really him?"

Louisa narrowed her eyes. "It certainly isn't a coincidence that the fissure in Berlin was over the bunker. It's very possible."

I shook my head. "What a freaking nightmare."

"Do you know the best way to defeat a nightmare?"

I shrugged. "Melatonin?"

"Hardly! That stuff will give you vivid nightmares. The best way to beat a nightmare is to wake up."

I snorted. "Well, this is a nightmare that's invaded the waking world. Fat chance of that."

Louisa patted my knee. "But when you wake up, your rational mind returns. That doesn't mean the fear goes away, but you can think through it and sort out the source of your fear, whatever birthed the nightmare to begin with. Then you can confront it and defeat it. Not by returning to the nightmare. But facing it on your terms, in your world."

"I have a recurring nightmare that my teeth are falling out. You're saying a trip to the dentist will solve it?"

Louisa smiled. "Perhaps it might. That's not an uncommon dream. Many times, so I hear, it happens if you're grinding your teeth at night. Do you know why people usually grind their teeth?"

"Not really."

"It's the result of stress. Going to the dentist might help protect your teeth, but it won't deal with the problem. You need to find a way to manage the stress."

"All right. Given what we're facing now, what's the metaphorical stress? What is it we have to face?"

"Pull out your wand."

"Louisa! That's not appropriate. I'm a married man."

Louisa smiled. "You're too young for me, sweetheart. I'm serious. This isn't a joke."

"But you warded the house."

"Pull out your wand, Thomas."

I retrieved Wand from my pocket. It still glowed green from the enchantment. The arcane power within still flowed. "I don't understand. Why isn't the ward silencing my power?"

"Because my ward only silences dark arcane power."

"I didn't know you could do that."

Louisa grinned. "Of course I can. Just as Hana and her mages managed to ward Berlin of pure arcane magic."

"She's using a domestic mage?" I asked.

"Perhaps. Though, from what I understand, Hana emerged from the deep with the ability to channel more than her natural gate magery. Perhaps she did it herself."

I raised my eyebrows. "A ward can be cast over an entire city?"

"With access to enough power, certainly. I imagine she needed the fissure in Berlin to pull it off. She can't do that here. Not yet."

"We don't have access to that much power. We can't open a fissure of our own. There'd be no way to pull out only pure energy without the dark power mingled with it."

"You don't need a fissure. You need more mages, as many as you can gather, to channel their power together. Every mage has something like a fissure within, an opening to the arcane wells."

"The ethereal organ?"

"Some call it that. As I understand, when you first saved the battlemages from the glacier, you combined the power of other mages to enhance the abilities of your empaths. You could do the same with a domestic mage. We could ward the entire city. Not just St. Louis. Berlin, as well."

I shook my head. "But Goebbels is already recruiting mages throughout the city."

"You have three empaths already willing to help. Mary, Jessie, and Rose. Fight his propaganda with some of your own. Not with deception, not by manipulating minds, but by channeling the truth. If Hana lures all the mages in the city to her side, she won't need a fissure. She'll draw what power she requires through the mages. Take that away from her."

"Dark energy is already leaking into the city," I pointed out. "Maybe not through a fissure, but through small pinholes into the arcane wells. That's what Elijah sensed before."

Louisa folded her hands in her lap. "Just enough to allow Goebbels to give everyone a taste, to tempt them, like an addictive drug that if someone touches once, they won't be able to stop using."

I nodded. "If we can hijack Goebbels' attempt to sway the American mages, Hana might have no other choice but to form another fissure."

"If she does that, you bring all the mages together and I will help you ward the city. With a ward in place silencing dark power, the only power anyone will be able to draw from her fissure will be pure power. You'll be able to take out Hana and the rest of her mages."

I chuckled. "And here I thought you were just a great cook."

Louisa laughed. "I've been around a long time, dear. I was just a young girl when the Entente alliance went underground. I've seen it all and lived through more than most."

Kat emerged from the boys' room and sat on the other side of me. She put her arm around me and kissed my cheek. "Let me guess, your *treat* is going to have to wait."

I kissed her back. "I'm taking a raincheck. I still expect that when I get home. For now, we have a plan. I need to get back to the alliance."

CHAPTER TWENTY-THREE

My phone still wasn't working. That EMP in Berlin had fried it. I was about to get in my truck to leave when Kat handed me her phone. Why didn't I think of that? A phone is sort of like underwear. Using someone else's just feels wrong. *Especially* if it's my wife's.

Hans and Jessie hadn't been in Berlin, so their phones would work. I sent them a text, and about a minute later a portal formed in my living room. I gave Kat her phone back and one more kiss before I left. I felt a little better with Louisa there. She could keep the ward viable and make sure Goebbels didn't mess with my son.

I hopped through the portal and appeared in the lunchroom. Most of the battlemages from Berlin were still resting, but Nigel was there with Hans, Jessie, Mary, and several other Entente mages. They were watching the same broadcast I was watching at home.

"What's this idea you had?" Nigel asked.

Jessie grinned. "I already know it."

I rolled my eyes. "Of course you do."

"It was Louisa's idea," Jessie explained. "She thinks if we work together, the empaths I mean, we might be able to counter Goebbels' recruitment efforts."

I nodded. "And if we can gather all the mages in the city, it may be enough power that Louisa can cast a ward over the whole city. One that silences dark power but allows us to operate."

Nigel pinched his chin. "That would leave the Axis mages powerless. We'd gain the advantage."

"That's the hope." I tried to sound confident. "There's still a wildcard, though. I'm not sure how Hana might still use her enchanted blade. We know she used it from within the ethereal realm to open the fissure in Gregory Park. I'm not sure if it will do anything if she uses it here."

"I need to talk to Evander," Hans said. "If it's gate magery at work, she may still be able to open the fissure again from this side. Even if she doesn't have access to dark power."

Nigel pressed his hands together and raised them to his lips. "The ward might still stop the dark power from blasting through the fissure."

I nodded. "It would only give us more pure arcane energy to wield."

"Who is to say that, because Hana uses dark magic, she *couldn't* use pure magic as well?" Jessie asked.

"She probably can," Nigel allowed. "Still, if that's the case, it will be a level battlefield. My guess is that Hana will only be able to use her natural gate magery. Anyone she's raised who had powers in life will likewise only be able to wield their original abilities."

Jessie considered this. "It still might take them a moment to feel it out, to discover what we've done."

"Provided Goebbels isn't reading our minds all the while," I added. "But even he won't have as much strength if his powers are limited and he can't access the darker part of the wells."

"He still has his power now," Nigel reminded me. "We must guard our thoughts. This is our plan. We don't speak of it again."

"To stand a chance against Goebbels, I will need Jessie and Rose both," Mary put in.

Hans looked concerned at this. "Are you sure my grandmother is up for it?"

We didn't have much choice, and Mary knew it. "Let's hope she is. This won't work without her. It would help if you were there with us, Hans. You can help keep her grounded and focused."

"What of all the pinholes Hana has created through the city?" Nigel asked. "We know dark power is leaking through."

"Louisa had a theory about that as well," I replied. "She believes that's what Goebbels is using to tempt the American mages. All he has to do is get them to touch the dark power once and he'll have them hooked."

Mary set her mouth in a grim line. "Then we'd better get started. Let's hope this works."

Nigel nodded. "If it does, we'll need Louisa and as many domestic mages as we can gather. We can all channel our energy together, but the domestic mages will be the ones who have to ward the city. The more we gather, the stronger the ward that Louisa and the domestic mages can cast. Every second we wait gives Goebbels more opportunity to recruit more mages to his cause."

I turned to Jessie. "Let us know when you have more mages en route. As many as we can gather. Until then, the battlemages from Berlin are resting. We may still need them at full strength to fight the Axis mages later."

Jessie nodded. "You need your rest as well, Tommy. We need you at full strength."

"She's right. Find a bed and get some shut-eye until everything is ready," Nigel insisted.

"What about you?" I asked.

"I'll be fine, mate. I'll get some rest if I can. You're the one with the enchanted wand. I'll make sure everything's in order."

"All of you should rest," Mary urged. "I can wake all of you in a second. I'll use my abilities. When we're ready, when we've recruited as many mages as we can, I'll let you know."

Hans left with Mary and Jessie. They were going to operate from Rose's room, where Hans' grandmother was most comfortable. That so much of our plan depended on an empath mage who suffered from dementia didn't inspire a ton of confidence. Still, Rose was doing a lot better than before. Mary and Jessie were working with her. Most of the time she was alert and well—but not all of the time.

I could do nothing. Jessie was right. I was pooped. I needed a little shut-eye if I was going to be ready to face Hana.

Chances were good that she'd try to reopen the fissure. She'd revert to her Plan A if we foiled her Plan B. Hopefully she didn't have a Plan C we weren't anticipating, but she probably did. Still, if she did try to open the fissure again, we'd know where to find her when the time came. Once we located her, provided the first step of our plan worked, we'd have to time everything perfectly. The gate mages would send us and all the battlemages to stop Hana in the park. The domestic mages would raise the ward before she and her Axis mages could tap into their power and attack, and that would be our window to strike. It was the best chance we had. Maybe the only chance we had.

As much as I wanted to stay up and help, there wasn't anything I could do yet. I wasn't sure I'd be able to sleep with so much going on in my mind. I was scared that if I slowed down I'd have no choice but to think about the battle we'd just been through and the one to come. What had Louisa said? The same thing Nigel told me when we were training with our sabers: I had to face my fear and overcome it. At the moment, that meant trying to get a little sleep.

CHAPTER TWENTY-FOUR

Alarm clock by empath mage isn't the most pleasant way to wake up from a deep sleep. It was like the time Kat set our Alexa to wake me up to the tune of *Barbie Girl*. There are few things I wanted to hear less when I was groggy and grumpy than that. Mary went for a classic alarm sound, that damn high-pitched repeated hybrid buzzing-beeping sound that old-school alarms used to use back in the day.

How long was I asleep? A couple of hours? It was still dark outside, so I didn't get a full night's sleep. I didn't own a watch, and I had a phone that didn't work anymore. I had no idea how much time had passed, but I was worried that if they were waking me so soon, the news wasn't great. It wouldn't take long to discern that Goebbels already had most of the mages lured to his side. It would take a lot longer for our empaths to reach out and convince the American mages to join us.

I was so out of it I nearly forgot that I was in my underwear. What little sleep I got wasn't nearly enough, as evidenced by the fact that I almost walked out into the hallways in my briefs. I hadn't had the "showing up at school in my underwear" nightmare since I was a teenager. Since the headquarters doubled as a school, I almost made that old nightmare a reality.

I slipped into my pants and shoes and scurried into the nearest bathroom to splash cold water on my face. It would have to do. This was as awake and alert as I was going to get. At least for now.

I assumed I was supposed to meet everyone back in the cafeteria, but when I got there it was empty. I heard footsteps approach and Jessie walked in alone.

"What's going on? Why did you wake me up? Did it work?"

Jessie bit her lip. "Mary and Rose are still working on the rest. We were able to convince about a third of the mages to join us. Another third were already lost. Goebbels got to them first."

"And the other third?"

"That's what Mary and Rose are doing now. I'll go back to join them shortly, but I thought you might want to get started. The mages we were able to reach are on their way here now."

"A third of the mages in the city. That's what? A dozen or so, give or take?"

"Fifteen in total. Here's the thing, Tommy. Most of them are young. Like Elijah, they heard Goebbels but were too afraid to listen to the voice. Oddly enough, it was older, more experienced mages that Goebbels managed to turn."

I shook my head. "He prioritized those who already had a mastery of their skills. I suspect he just hadn't gotten to the children yet."

"The third we're still working on are more experienced. I need to get back to help. Goebbels is working on them. It's a real contest, a competition for their minds."

"Don't stick around talking to me, then," I urged. "Get back and help. I'm glad we managed to save the children. It might also be harder to focus their energy to do what must be done."

"It may have to do. Don't underestimate them, Tommy. All they need to do is channel their natural power so that Louisa and the domestic mages in the alliance can wield it to form the barrier. They don't need to focus their energies."

"And these children are making their way here alone?"

Jessie shook her head. "Hans and Evander are gathering them. They'll arrive by portal any moment now."

"And their parents?"

"Some of them are already allied with the Axis mages. These children are going to help save their parents."

I shook my head. "I can't imagine my son being in that position."

"He should come, along with Louisa. We need everyone we can get, and your son has a lot of raw power."

I smiled widely. "Yeah, he has great mage genes."

"Unfortunately, humility is a recessive trait in your family," she shot back.

I smiled. "I'm humble. I'm one of the most humble people I know!"

Jessie rolled her eyes. "That was a joke, wasn't it?"

I chuckled. "You know it was. Get back with Mary and Rose. Do your thing. I'll be ready when the young mages arrive."

Jessie took off back through the halls to join the other empaths. I wasn't sure how I was going to handle this. I love my kids, and I'm good with *my* kids. It sounds bad to say, but I always found other people's kids difficult. I wouldn't go so far as to say I didn't like kids. I just wasn't good with them.

Some people had a way of talking to kids, getting through to them. They could keep a room full of kids calm and on task. That wasn't me. I might be able to lead a bunch of grown mages into battle. Leading a bunch of tweens, though? Well, that was a hell of a lot more intimidating.

I headed into the kitchen. The domestic mages who worked in the cafeteria always had cookies on hand. I pulled a Tupperware container from one of the pantries and set it on the counter.

That was my strategy for dealing with them. Give them cookies and hope for the best.

I really could have used Jessie. She was great with kids, probably because she knew their thoughts and could feel their prepubescent angst. Jessie was understandably occupied, though, and I was going to have to do this.

Hans and Evander couldn't deliver them all at once. They had to go from house to house. That meant the crowd would start small. I had a chance. Dealing with one or two at a time wasn't that intimidating.

A portal appeared and Hans showed up with a girl of maybe sixteen with long dark hair. About fifteen seconds later, another portal delivered another girl of about the same age with red curls. Evander and Hans didn't waste any time, but quickly formed portals and left again.

I carried the cookies over to a table. "Want one?"

The dark-haired girl rolled her eyes. "Cookies? That's so lame."

"Totally," the redhead added. "Our parents are probably freaking out right now."

"Mine don't give a shit," the dark-haired girl mumbled. "They won't even notice I'm gone until tomorrow. I'm Anna, by the way." She took a cookie from the tub.

I smiled. "I'm Tom."

"I'm Nikki," the redhead said. She grabbed a cookie and took a small bite. "Oh my God! These are great."

"See. Cookies aren't so lame after all, are they?"

Anna shrugged. "My mom's are just as good. She's a domestic. So am I."

"What about you, Nikki?"

"Battlemage. I blow shit up."

I chuckled. "That's something I can relate to."

Anna took another bite. "So our parents got recruited by Nazis?"

I nodded. "More or less. It's a little more complicated than that. Their empath can be persuasive. I doubt they realize who they're aligned with."

Nikki snorted. "Nazis are so lame. What is this, an Indiana Jones movie?"

I tilted my head. "You know Indiana Jones? Those movies are great."

"Those movies suck," Nikki offered in reply. "My dad is obsessed with them. I don't get it."

I pressed my lips together, suppressing my urge to accuse the girl of heresy. How could anyone think Indiana Jones *sucked*? That man was the hero of my youth. "The mages we're facing aren't like the Nazis from the movies. They're dark mages. Most of them were dead, raised again through necromancy. I need your help to stop them. To defeat them and save your parents before they do anything they'll regret. The dark magic that the bad guys are using to tempt them is addicting."

Nikki raised an eyebrow. "The bad guys? That's so dramatic."

I narrowed my eyes. "Would you prefer villains?"

The two girls exchanged glances and eye rolls. "Look, mister," Anna began. "I don't know about Nazis or villains. But if these people are screwing with our parents, well, I'll do whatever I can to kick their asses."

"You're a domestic," Nikki pointed out. "How are you going to kick their asses?"

Anna grinned. "I'll bake them shit pies."

I smiled. "Actually, domestic mages are exactly what we need. We're going to ward the city against their dark power. I know you probably don't know how to do that, but you won't be alone."

"What about me?" Nikki asked. "I can fight. I've got skills."

"For now, all we need is to focus everyone's power together. My hope is you won't have to fight."

"Screw that," Nikki snapped. "I'm a battlemage. Kicking ass is what I was born to do."

I smiled. "You and me both, kid. Do you have wands?"

Nikki and Anna both pulled their wands out and set them on the table.

I nodded. "I can't help you much, Anna. But Nikki, while we wait, ever form your wand into a lightsaber? You know, like Luke Skywalker?"

Nikki raised an eyebrow. "Skywalker? You're so old. I want to be like Rey."

I swallowed the urge to argue the superiority of the original franchise over the newer films. "All right. Just like Rey. Want me to show you how to do it?"

"Hells yeah!" I wasn't sure why she pluralized 'hell,' but I got the gist. This was just a start. More young mages were bound to arrive soon. Why not get this one started on the right foot? Young folk were like lemmings. If I had these two mages following my lead by the time others showed up, the rest would follow.

Nikki was a natural. She summoned her saber on the second try. It had taken me five or six attempts before I got it right.

"Impressive. Now, the trick is to learn how to wield it. That takes practice. I'm still learning, myself."

Nikki spun with her saber. She did a little flip and swung it in the air as if she already knew what she was doing.

All I could do was laugh. "I see you have a little training."

Nikki added. "Martial arts. Been training since I was eight. I know what to do with this. You have to let me fight!"

I wasn't sure what to say. I didn't want to discourage her enthusiasm. At the same time, sending a sixteen-year-old into a battle wasn't something I could allow in good conscience unless we had no other choice. I hoped it wouldn't come to that—but deep down I suspected it might.

CHAPTER TWENTY-FIVE

It only took a couple of hours for Hans and Evander to gather the rest. The youngest of the mage recruits was twelve. The oldest was barely twenty. They'd all manifested, but some of the younger mages hadn't specialized. The rest were battlemages and domestic mages. No gate mages or empaths were among them, which wasn't a surprise. Battlemagery and domestic magery were the most common specializations passed on from generation to generation among American mages.

While Hans and Evander were portaling the young mages, Jessie, Marie, and Rose were still working hard to recruit others. They managed to convince five more to join us, including my parents. Hans left to retrieve Louisa and Elijah while Evander went to pick up my parents and the others.

Seeing my mother and father arrive was a major relief. My mother's power, added to Louisa's and the other domestics in the alliance, gave me hope that we might be able to pull off the plan.

As good as it was to see them and know they hadn't been lured by Goebbels, they came with baggage. My parents were always critical of my decisions as a mage. They weren't bad parents. They supported me, and I grew up in a loving household. They also had impossibly high standards that, in their eyes, I always fell short of. I could save the freaking world and they'd pull me aside to tell me how I could have done a better job of it, where I might have made better choices and saved more lives. They didn't mean to be cruel about it. Their motives were pure. They wanted me to be the best I could be. That meant, as my father often put it, never settling for "good enough." Always finding room to grow, never satisfied with imperfect success. It made me stronger. It also took an emotional toll. Nothing I wasn't used to, but nothing I wanted to deal with at the moment. I had so much pressure on my shoulders already, and I didn't know how much more I could take before the weight would crush me.

Jessie sensed my anxiety and kept them distracted while I welcomed the other mages. I waved at my parents and my mother waved back. My father nodded at me. I nodded back. Nigel gathered the rest of the alliance mages and met us in the cafeteria.

When Hans got back with Louisa and Elijah, my son ran over to me and hugged me. "I get to help?"

I ruffled my fingers over his shaggy head. "Just like before. When we channeled our power together to help Jessie find the battlemages. This time we're channeling the power to Louisa."

"Easy peasy!"

I smiled. "You'll have to stay here with her and the others. They may need more power to keep the wards strong. I'll have to leave to fight. Be strong, son."

Elijah smiled at me. "I've got this, Dad."

Nigel brought the rest of the alliance into the cafeteria, and from the looks on everyone's faces, he wasn't anyone's favorite person at the moment. He had woken up every mage in the place in the middle of the night. It's a wonder someone didn't blast him in the butt with an arcane missile.

"Everyone join hands," I shouted. "Those of you who haven't

done this, we'll be pooling our magic and allowing our domestic mages to use it to ward the whole city. At least as much of the city as we can cover. When you feel the power flowing through your hands, add your own to it. Once the shields are up, we'll move fast. Our empaths believe they'll be able to sense the enemy once the wards are up and all the dark power is muted. Evander will form a portal, and those of us trained for battle will go through."

"What qualifies as training, son?" my mother asked.

I grunted. Until then, most of the mages didn't realize that was my mom. "Battlemages who are of age. Portal mages will also be useful in the battle. Jessie will be coming. One empath is helpful in battle."

"What's 'of age'?" Nikki asked.

"If you're too young to sign up for the secular military, you shouldn't go to war. Stay here and protect the home base. We still need a few here to stand guard, a reserve force just in case."

Nigel cleared his throat. "That includes any mages with physical conditions that make joining a battle untenable. All domestics will stay here, and their combined energy should be enough to maintain the ward once it's up."

"Bottom line is, I won't force anyone to fight. We can use every capable wand we have. Still, it's your choice at the end of the day. We don't have time to test everyone's strength. If you think you have the vigor to fight and you are willing, join us. We need you. If you think you'd be a liability, or if you're untrained and young, remain here. You're still needed. As a portal mage, Hana Sato will still have her original natural abilities. She could still drop a small force here. I do not anticipate she will, but we need to be ready for any contingency. I'd take questions, but we don't have time for that. Louisa, are you ready?"

Louisa nodded. "I am."

Everyone joined hands. It didn't take long before the flow of energy swelled in my hands. That much power passing through all of us, like a current, was intense. It wasn't painful. The sensation was almost euphoric. Elijah giggled a little as he squeezed my hand. It was pure magic. No one was channeling anything remotely dark into the arcane circuit.

The domestic mages were all gathered on either side of Louisa, straight across the circle from me. The series of domestics on either side of Louisa functioned a lot like a wand, their successive energies focused the raw power that coursed through the rest of us into the shape that domestic mages used. By the time it reached Louisa, she was prepared to either ward the city from dark magic or clean everyone's house at once. As much as many might have appreciated the latter, I was pretty sure she was sticking to the original plan.

Wards were powerful, but not especially impressive by appearance. Most domestic magery was less than flashy but immensely practical. Far more useful than battlemagery ninety-nine percent of the time. When there wasn't a war or magical battle going on, my skills were mostly useless. A lot of young people don't understand that. Everyone who manifests *hopes* to specialize in battlemagery or portal magery. Hardly anyone wants to be a domestic mage. In the long run, though, on the usefulness scale, the inverse was true.

Imagine never having to scrub dishes, or toilets, or pick up your kids' toys. What if you had gourmet meals all the time, and hardly had to lift a finger to pull it off? Would you turn that down for the ability to kick ass now and then?

Still, when we were needed, when someone threatened civilization, battlemages were heroes. We put everything on the line.

Louisa looked across the circle at me and nodded. That meant it was done. We had no way to know how far it expanded from where we were. Presumably, though, it covered most of the city, including Gregory Park.

Jessie broke rank from the circle, and I did the same. Jessie pressed the tip of her wand to her temple. "Let's hope this works."

I watched and waited, my heart racing a little with anticipation, as Jessie squinted, pursed her lips, and tilted her head to one side and then the other. I had no idea what it was like to search a city with an empath's abilities. I always envisioned it as soaring over a city in virtual reality, scanning the world below, and picking up any mages based on the magic that emanated from their spirits. It was probably nothing like that. The idea, though, wasn't far off. If there were mages who weren't shrouded by dark power, she could find them. With the darker magic warded and some kind of threshold of evilness affecting the ward's tolerance, it was theoretically possible to find Hana. Then again, since she didn't have a regular body, we weren't sure. At the very least, we knew the mages who she'd recruited. They weren't entirely corrupted. Even without the ward, we had a good chance of locating them.

Jessie lowered her wand. "They aren't all there, but it looks like several mages are moving toward Gregory Park."

"Can you hear any of their thoughts?"

Jessie nodded. "I can, but trying to tap into all of them will take time. If Hana is going to make a fissure, well, it won't take her as long as it does others to get there. She might already be working on it."

I waved Evander over. We'd decided to keep Hans at the headquarters since Hana targeted him before. We also thought it might be better to leave him there to help people evacuate if the Axis mages attacked.

"We need a large portal to Gregory Park," I instructed Evander. "Make it large enough that we can move in quickly. We don't want to funnel in there one-by-one defenseless. They could pick us off as we went through."

Evander grinned. "Not a problem."

Waving his wand in a large circle, Evander formed a portal that he suspended just a few inches away from the far wall. It was large enough that every mage in the place could move through at once.

Nigel moved all the mages into an attack formation, with battlemages up front. We had a few portal mages, including Evander, who we kept behind the rest. They could move forces around the battlefield, dropping portals over mage's heads and sending them into strategic positions. We hadn't had that advantage in Berlin.

I moved to the front with Nigel.

"Ready, mate?"

I nodded and formed my arcane saber at the end of my wand before turning to the rest of the mages. "Remember! Strike first. Strike hard. No mercy!"

Hans wasn't going with us, but he laughed and shook his head. "That's Cobra Kai, dude. Not exactly the most admirable tactic."

I shrugged and raised my voice over the crowd. "Right now, a Cobra Kai–style attack is what's required. If we don't take Hana down now, we might not get another shot. My wand alone can take her down. Have my back. Evander will move me into position when it's safe and she's vulnerable. Remember, some of these mages are not wholly to blame. They've been warped by Goebbels and dark magic. They're also the families and parents of some of the mages here. The goal is not to wipe *them* out, but to clear a path so I can take Hana out. We need to remove Goebbels from the scene as well if he shows his face."

It wasn't a super inspiring speech. Not like the one Nigel gave in Berlin. It was practical, though, which was more my style. Getting everyone in an emotional frenzy wasn't what this fight required. We had to fight smart, try not to kill the innocent, and focus on the goal. Hana and any undead mages were fair game. Could we get to them without having to fight through the flesh-and-blood American mages Goebbels recruited? We wouldn't know until we got there.

Jessie grabbed my hand. "I'll stay in the back. Keep your mind open. I may be able to reach out to you if I sense anything that might help."

I nodded and gave Jessie a friendly hug. "Be careful back there."

"You too, Tommy. We need you. Your family needs you. Follow your own advice. Fight smart."

I nodded, gripped my wand with the saber still formed on the end, and pointed it toward Evander's portal. "Mages! Move out!"

CHAPTER TWENTY-SIX

We appeared in the parking lot next to Gregory Park, but Hana had already sorted out what we were doing. One of her mages cast an arcane barrier around her and a dozen or more other mages in the middle of the park. Without the aid of dark magic, though, there wasn't any reason to believe we couldn't take the barrier down. We had a lot of firepower, and a barrier like that can only take so much arcane damage before it dissolves.

Jessie indicated more mages were coming, mostly the mages Goebbels had recruited through his arcane-powered propaganda. They were the ones we were most concerned about. They were the mages we didn't want to kill. The others were dead already. Killing the dead isn't murder. It's putting things back where they belong. My wand could do it.

The rest of the battlemages focused on Hana's barrier. It's not easy to see through a barrier, and the magic can be deceptive. Curved over her, the effect of the barrier also warped their sizes and shapes. Still, I was pretty sure that she didn't have more than a dozen mages inside. Given the size of the army we'd faced before, I imagined she had a much larger force in waiting, and not all of them would be flesh-and-blood. We just didn't know how many dead mages she had raised between the time she left Berlin and when we arrived back in St. Louis.

Behind the barrier, Hana had an advantage. What was she doing in there? I couldn't tell. Her mages weren't fighting back, though, and my best guess was that they were going to reopen the fissure. They weren't fighting, because they were focused on that and hoping it would be too many for our ward to handle.

We could bust through the barrier and all it would take was a single gate for Hana to run away. If that was her plan, though, why were reinforcements on the way? She didn't know for sure if she had enough time to complete what she was doing. She needed a distraction, something to take some of our battlemages' fire and divert it from the barrier. She was buying time, and we had to make sure she didn't get it.

We charged Hana and her barrier, blasting it with arcane missiles. I hoped my enchantment might knock it out straight-away, but Hana was wielding pure energy. There was nothing abhorrent about the magic she was using.

She wasn't doing much inside the barrier. One of her other mages was channeling power to sustain it. She was simply watching us approach from a distance. Her calmness and lack of anxiety about our attack disturbed me. It meant she had another plan.

I didn't see Goebbels inside, and I didn't recognize any of the other mages beside Hana. A couple of them wore SS uniforms. They might have been the same mages we defeated in Berlin, raised again along with Hana to rejoin her effort.

Hana had her wand in hand. She wouldn't stay there long enough for us to take down the barrier. She'd portal herself somewhere else —anywhere else—and we'd be back to square one, trying to track her down. If she gated outside the ward, what was stopping her from reconnecting with her dark power and forming another fissure?

I raised my hand. "Cease fire!"

"What are you doing?" Nigel asked.

"I'm going to talk to her."

"What good is that going to do?"

I shook my head. "I don't know. But my gut tells me this isn't going to work."

"We still have to try!"

"Give me a few seconds. That's all."

I approached the edge of the barrier. I could cast a barrier over hers and her portals wouldn't be able to get past. If she was doing something inside there, though, all I'd do was give her more time to finish the job. I needed to find out what she was doing.

"What is your plan here, Hana?"

Hana looked at me with her dark eyes. She looked younger than the last time I saw her. She wasn't in her actual body anymore, but in a form of her own making, a projection of her mind knit together through arcane energies. "What are you doing here, Tommy? I have to hand it to you. I didn't expect you back for nearly another day. How did you do it?"

I laughed. My enchantment, the spell Irene had cast in Berlin, was my only ace up my sleeve. I wasn't about to tell her the truth. "I'd tell you, but then I'd have to kill you."

"Just like when we were kids. You still use humor to deflect."

I shrugged. "I'd take humor over murder any day of the week. Perhaps you could try your hand at a joke or two. I'll even give you a courtesy laugh."

Hana shook her head. "What are you going to do, Tommy? Destroy the barrier? Cast another one over mine to stop me from casting a portal away from here?"

I sniffed and wiped my nose. "It crossed my mind."

Hana rolled her black eyes. "Predictable. It doesn't matter what you do. Even if you killed me, well, I'm already dead. I can come back again."

"Your enchantment only forms a fissure in the park. If you come back, I'll kill you again."

"Around and around we go. It would be a waste of your energies. Besides, once the dark power is unleashed again and overpowers your pitiful ward, you won't be able to kill me. I have powers you haven't even considered."

"Drop that barrier and we'll see about that."

"That's always been your weakness. You're powerful, I'll give you that. I used to envy you, you know? It was youthful foolishness. You've always overestimated your abilities."

"Have I?" I raised an eyebrow. "You're the one with a vision to merge the arcane and material worlds. What makes you think you can pull that off? What if the world you create isn't what you expect? Hans is safe. He's happy. Your son is a good man. More than that, he doesn't want this world you're trying to make."

She narrowed her eyes at me. "I know what you're doing. You think if I feel peace, my spirit will be put to rest. It's clever, I'll give you that. I've been dead a long time. If I were a wandering spirit who never knew death, perhaps your strategy would work. There's only one thing that will give me peace, now, though."

"By merging the realms? That would give you peace?"

"By making sure that no matter what happens, Hans won't have to languish in the ethereal realm. The only way I can give him peace, the only way I can ensure he's safe, is to defeat the one thing that threatens everyone. To put an end to death itself."

"It won't end up the way you hope. It won't give you peace."

"Maybe my spirit can't be appeased. Perhaps I'll never find peace. I can live with that."

I looked past Hana. Her barrier made it hard to see exactly what the mages behind her were up to. They were doing *something*. What could they possibly do in such a small space, without access to dark magic? I gripped my wand. I had to be ready to cast a barrier before she could forge a portal. "It doesn't have to be that way, Hana. You could give up this deluded nightmare.

That you're back from the dead is a miracle already. What if you gave up this fool's game? You could get to know your son. You could help us make the world better as it is."

Hana shook her head. "All the while, the specter of death would loom over all of us."

"You're afraid of peace. You're scared that if you got to know Hans, if you saw how happy he was, it would give you peace. This isn't about saving him from death. It's all about *your* fear. You're afraid of being trapped in the ethereal realm again, restless for eternity."

Hana grunted. "It doesn't matter. You still can't stop me."

"I'm prepared to do exactly that!"

"The ward was clever. I'll give you that. You forgot one thing."

"What did I forget?" I demanded.

"The ward only guards this world. Do you really think I raised every spirit from the ethereal realm to fight here? There are thousands more, still waiting for their liberation, who can access all the dark power that the wells can offer. I'm sure you've already noticed that I've pierced a thousand holes all around the city between the realms."

"The dark energy won't escape those leaks under the ward."

"Who said I needed it to escape? What do you say we test the strength of your ward?"

"I can't let you do that, Hana!"

Hana smirked. "Try and stop me."

Her wand assumed a blue glow. Before she could cast her gate, I formed a barrier over hers.

She didn't form a portal. Not out of the barrier. She formed one at her feet. She couldn't forge a gate to escape. What was she doing? The mages inside her barrier blasted magic into her gate, and the gate itself turned dark as the power from the other side, from the deeper wells, pressed against it. It couldn't get through.

Arcane energy filled the air like electricity. I turned and saw a series of small patches in the ground glowing blue, but as I watched, they turned dark and violent. The patches couldn't be any larger than a golf ball. They were the pinhole leaks, and they were all over the park and on the roads beyond, probably scattered across the city.

Cracks of violet energy spread from each patch, spiderwebbing from one miniature fissure to the next.

I quickly dropped my barrier and yelled, "Hit her with everything you've got!"

The battlemages all unleashed arcane missiles at Hana's barrier, and I did the same. The land all around us shook. The energy wasn't escaping the cracks. The ward was holding it in. Hana's dead mages were attacking every fissure, every pinhole that pierced the divide between realms, and they were doing it from *inside* the ethereal realm.

I knew that every ward had its limitations, defined by the power that cast it. That didn't mean one mage could overwhelm a single domestic mage's ward. A mage within the ward couldn't access power, so he wouldn't have any ability to counter the ward. Wards weren't like barriers, either. You could fire into a ward, but the ward would dispel any missiles or anything else shot into it.

That was the only way I knew that a ward might fail, and it took a lot of mages. The exact number was probably somewhere in the vicinity of a shit ton. Apologies to those on the metric system. I'm not sure of the equivalent term. A bloody load, perhaps.

That was what it took to take down a ward cast by a single domestic mage. The ward our mages made was exponentially stronger. Could it hold a network, a spiderweb of energies? We weren't dealing with a single fissure but an entire network of dark energy coursing through the ground.

We showered Hana's barrier with blast after blast. It was working, but I wasn't sure it would be fast enough. So many factors were at play. What if the arcane cracks in the ground overwhelmed the ward just as we dropped Hana's barrier? We'd be in for a real fight, much like the battle in Berlin.

It was difficult to focus. The cracks in the ground, connecting one pinhole from the ethereal realm to the next, were expanding. It was like the pinholes had perforated the divide between realms, and all it would take was a blast from the other side to rip it apart.

The way the ground shifted under my feet, I was afraid the whole park was about to sink into the arcane wells.

Hana's barrier flickered like a light bulb about to burn out. We almost had it down.

A shower of arcane missiles blasted at us from the opposite direction. The American mages, under Goebbel's influence, had arrived.

Nigel cast a barrier over us as Hana stood beneath her failing shield laughing. As her shield faded away, she cast a portal over herself and disappeared, leaving a dozen more undead mages behind.

They fired at us from their position. Their attacks struck Nigel's shield as the other mages attacked from the opposite side of the park.

"We need to regroup!" I screamed.

Nigel nodded and shouted at Evander, but I couldn't hear what he said. Evander formed a large portal and the battlemages fled through it.

"Let me through your barrier!" I shouted.

"Why?" Nigel asked.

"Just do it!"

Nigel pulled back some of the magic from one side of his barrier. I stepped out and aimed my wand at the undead mages.

The enchantment on my wand worked. The mage's bodies withered on contact. I waved my wand in an arc, blasting the crowd with a scattershot. It worked. At least we wouldn't have to worry about leaving them behind.

What would my wand do to them? Would it free them, purge the dark magic from their systems? Irene had told me the enchantment would restore order and set things right, but that was an unspecific and broad description of what the magic might do. I couldn't know for sure.

I lobbed a few cherry bombs in their direction, concussive blasts that might affect a few of them at once.

Where they struck, the mages didn't die but fell to their knees, clinging to their skulls. The others retreated.

The battlemages fled through a portal under Nigel's barrier. I found the weak spot Nigel had opened for me and pushed myself through again.

"You're going to leave them like that?" Nigel asked.

"I'm not sure what it did."

"It worked," Jessie crowed. "They're free of Goebbels' influence. I can't say they're ready to join us. All I sense is a lot of confusion and disorientation."

"Can you try and reach out to them from our headquarters?"

Jessie nodded. "With Mary's help, I believe I can."

"Let's get out of here. We need to lend our power to the domestic mages again. I'm not sure how long these wards will hold if we don't."

CHAPTER TWENTY-SEVEN

We made it back to the headquarters, and one look out the window told me everything I needed to know. The spiderwebs of arcane power were *everywhere.*

Nigel and the other mages who went with us rejoined the circle to support Louisa. We needed to strengthen this ward as much as possible. Once the ward failed, I had a feeling the ground under the city would explode in a massive bomb of arcane power. It would level the city. I didn't know for sure, but from the looks of it, and how the ground shook back at the park, it was a reasonable deduction. Louisa's ward was like the boy's finger in the hole of the dike, holding back the flood to save his city.

While the other mages formed a circle, I flipped on the television. *Massive Earthquake Rocks St. Louis* scrolled across the bottom of the screen.

Seismologists would likely be as stumped by this "earthquake" as they were about Berlin. It was just a matter of time before folks started marching out on the streets with signs declaring that the end was nigh. It didn't take a genius to realize that what was happening was more than an earthquake. Not that St. Louis didn't have them from time to time. More than two centuries ago, an earthquake along the New Madrid fault was so intense it forced the Mississippi to flow backward for three days.

Given what had happened in Berlin just days before, and the lack of credible scientific explanation, it wouldn't take long before the doomsayers latched onto it. They wouldn't be entirely wrong, either. What Hana was planning *was* an end of the world of a sort. Merging the realms of the living and the dead, the arcane and the mundane, would change life as everyone knew it. Things would never be the same. Hana presumed that freeing the dead would make death itself obsolete. What if it was exactly the opposite? What if merging the realms made *life* obsolete? What if the realm of the dead, the ethereal plane, swallowed up the world so that what we knew as life was little more than a drop of honey in an ocean of vinegar?

I needed to know how far these cracks spread beyond the city. Was there a pattern to them that we couldn't see from here that might be obvious from above?

I pulled Hans aside. "I need you to take me up into the sky."

"What are you talking about?"

"A portal up high above the city. So I can see what we're really dealing with."

Hans tilted his head. "I can send you through a series of portals into the sky. You can't fly, though. I'll have to gate you back to Earth again before you fall to the ground."

I nodded. "I understand that. I have a feeling, though, that my wand is the key to all of this. The enchantment is supposed to fix things, to set them right. I need to know what we're facing before I can even try to do something like that."

Hans chuckled and shook his head. "I thought you didn't like heights."

"I don't. But what choice do we have?"

"The news will probably get us a view from the sky, like they did in Berlin."

I shook my head. "We can't wait around watching television, depending on reporters for information. Whatever they might show us won't be the full picture."

"You have balls, Tom. I'll give you that."

I grinned. "I prefer to call it testicular fortitude."

"Follow me. We can start on the roof."

"Is there a hatch or something to get up there?"

Hans chuckled. "I don't know. I have gates, duh. It's probably best not to send you off again in front of everyone. Especially not in front of your son."

I felt a tug on my hand. It was Elijah. "Daddy, what's happening?"

I grabbed my boy's hand and squeezed. "I'm not sure yet. I'm going to find out. You should join the circle. Louisa and the domestics could still use all the power we can channel."

Elijah shook his head. "I heard what you told Hans. I want to go with you."

"I don't know if that's a good idea."

"If he's making gates like that, I might be able to do something like that one day. I want to see how it works."

I looked at Hans. He shrugged his shoulders. I didn't need his approval, and one more mage channeling power to the circle wasn't all that significant, all things considered. Still, Hans was going to have to watch him while I went hurling through the sky above. "You okay with it, Hans?"

"I'm fine with it if you are. You realize, Elijah, without a wand, you might not be able to cast gates like this. Not yet, anyway."

Elijah shrugged. "Maybe, maybe not. I can do more than you know."

"I'm not doubting your capabilities," Hans assured him. "Trying to do too much before you're ready, though, could be a mistake. It would take a lot out of you."

"I didn't say I'm going to do it. I just want to see how it's done. Please, Daddy?"

I patted Elijah on the top of his head. "All right. Come with us. Just promise me you'll watch from a distance. Don't bother Hans while he's casting. He'll need all his focus for this to work."

Elijah smiled widely. "I get it. I won't bug anyone. I just want to watch."

"You should go ask your mother."

"Mom isn't here."

I sighed. "I know. That's not the point. Do you know how much trouble I'd be in if she found out I let you go up on the roof?"

"I'll be *fine*, Dad! Please!"

I took a deep breath. "All right. Don't make me regret this."

We walked out into the hall, out of the view of the other mages, and Hans made a portal. I held Elijah's hand and stepped through it. We reappeared on the roof of the headquarters building and Hans came through right behind us.

From the roof, I could see several violet cracks of dark arcane energy running through the city streets. Some of them passed through buildings. They were pulsing erratically. Dead mages on the other side were probably still at work, blasting the cracks from their side, trying to overpower our ward.

"Are you sure you want to do this?" Hans asked.

I nodded. "I need to see everything."

Elijah tugged at my arm. "I can feel it again."

"You can feel what?"

"The dark power. Like I sensed it before. It's starting to leak through again."

I bit my lip and turned to Hans. "That means our ward is weakening. We have to figure this out before it's too late. If something happens, if the cracks break forth, can I trust you to get my son to safety?"

"If I'm not here to make more gates, Tom, you'll fall to the earth."

I nodded. "If the fissures blast open, don't worry about me. Promise me you'll keep my boy safe."

Hans sighed. "All right. I promise. After I make you another gate to make sure you can land on the ground without becoming a splat of human roadkill on the streets."

"If you have to choose between one or the other, save him. Not me."

Hans nodded. "It won't come to that."

I took a deep breath. "All right. Let's do this."

Hans pulled a portal down over my head. I emerged in the clouds, and my ears immediately pressurized. It hurt like hell. Should have seen that coming.

The wind against my face was intense as my body hurled toward the ground. When I passed the clouds, what I saw took away what little breath I had left.

The spiderweb of arcane cracks extended well beyond the city, far beyond our ward. Still, every crack eventually led to a center: Gregory Park. Whatever Hana's mages were doing behind her portal must've been the catalyst, the origin point. Hana couldn't cast dark magic under our ward, so she used what remained of the fissure to spread the power out to all the other small breaches she'd seeded across St. Louis and beyond.

Irene told me my enchanted wand could heal a fissure. What if I blasted the center, the origin point?

I was so high up in the sky that I didn't know how long it would take to fall. I'd seen enough. I was ready for another portal to take me back.

The energy from the fissures everywhere pulsed and blasted into the sky. It overwhelmed the ward.

Still no portal. I looked back toward the top of the headquarters. Hans was aiming his wand at me, but nothing was happening.

The released energies nullified his power. I was falling fast.

The only mages among us attuned to the ethereal realms were

battlemages. There wasn't anything they could do. I could try to form an arcane shield around me. I'd never used one like that before. Not to mention, I could move through my own barriers. Even with a shield, chances were good I'd go splat.

What we needed was a gate mage who could tap into the dark power, the ethereal magic pouring from the arcane wells.

As my body hurled toward the ground, I looked at my son. I wished I could have seen my whole family, but if the last thing I saw alive was my son, I'd call that a good way to go.

Elijah ran to the edge of the roof and a blast of power emanated from his hands. I gasped. I couldn't believe it. It made sense. He could sense the dark power from the beginning. Without a wand, his abilities were less refined and less focused. He was raw. That was exactly what he needed to harness the power in the air, though. I could only hope that the darkness wouldn't corrupt him. I wasn't sure if I was more proud or worried.

A portal formed just below me, and I fell right into it.

I didn't emerge back on top of the building. I emerged in darkness. Violet energy was all around me.

Elijah saved me, and I didn't go splat in the street. He sent me straight into the ethereal realm, though. It probably wasn't what he intended, but tapping into that power must've created an exit point for his gate inside the arcane wells.

Several figures approached from a distance. They glowed with a combination of blue and violet energies. I gripped Wand. He glowed green with Irene's enchantment. Would that be enough to fight off an entire army of dead mages?

Flight wasn't an option. I could allow Wand to pull me to the fissure, but these other mages were moving so fast they'd catch up to me before I could escape. If I went back through the portal behind me, I'd end up back in the sky, falling to my death. My only chance to live was to fight.

CHAPTER TWENTY-EIGHT

All I could see were the outlines of the spirit mages as they drew nearer, but I could not make out their faces. I wasn't about to wait for them to swarm around me. I didn't know what they'd do to me, but I was in the ethereal realm with my body. Was my body real there? How can you have a body in a non-material realm? I guessed that my body took an astral form. Why it didn't work before, I wasn't sure. I was able to do it when I buried our dead in Berlin. There were two possibilities.

Either I lacked the focus to pull off going astral while hurling toward the earth, which was a likely possibility given the adrenaline flowing through my body on account of my fear of heights.

Or however Hana pulled off the blast of ethereal power through the webbed series of fissures, this was different from what happened in Berlin. Maybe it neutralized my magic this time, too, despite my having been to the ethereal realm.

There was also a third possibility. The ability to access magic in an ethereal environment wasn't a permanent gift. Perhaps it wore out over time, or I had a certain amount of compatible magic that I could use, and I'd used it all in Berlin.

Whatever the case, my son saved my life. For the time being. I wasn't about to let these dead mages "recruit" me to their company.

I had to get back to my son, to all my family. Elijah was probably scared to death. He tried to save me, and I disappeared. Did he think he'd killed me? If he didn't know he'd saved me, he must have been in a panic. Hans couldn't protect him. Did we have any mages who could still wield their powers? The only thing I'd tried to do was take an astral form. I hadn't thought to test anything else.

Wand still glowed with green energy, and it came to life in the ethereal realm. A mage's wand was born in an ethereal dimension. Not this one, specifically, or at least not in this particular section, if you could call it that. The principles that governed this realm, though, resonated within Wand. Why it was more vigorous here, and why most mages' magic was silenced when Hana released the energies of this realm to earth, was due to the specific *kind* of arcane magic she drew out of the fissures.

Irene's enchantment was the wildcard. How would an Earth-based magic function in a realm where there wasn't any Earth? I was about to find out.

I spun Wand overhead and released a scattershot of green blasts at the approaching crowd. The dark power within them turned to a green hue that matched my enchantment. What did that mean? Did they merely absorb some of the power, or did it change them somehow?

All I knew was that the spirit armies continued encroaching on my position, moving steadily in my direction.

When they got close, I recognized one of them. I rubbed my eyes to make sure it wasn't an illusion.

"Gerhard Wagner?"

Hans' grandfather smiled back at me. "Thank you for the drink. It was refreshing to consume the flavor of the earth again."

I tilted my head. "Y'all aren't coming at me to kill me?"

Gerhard shook his head. "Not at all."

I huffed. "I figured you all would be on board with Hana Sato. She wants to merge the arcane realms with Earth. She thinks it will end death once and for all."

Gerhard made a sound that mimicked the clearing of one's throat. Did he actually have a throat? If he did, he had an ethereal frog in it. "Why would we want that?"

I shrugged. "I don't know. To be alive again?"

Gerhard tilted his head. "Death is not suffering. It is not pain. Only a restless spirit, one who cannot let go of something in the world, would imagine something like that is desirable."

I scratched my head. "I thought about that. Her son isn't her unresolved issue. She claims that death itself is her anxiety. The only way she can find peace is to erase the divide between life and death, to merge the realms."

"Death is not her unresolved issue," another voice said. "I am."

I turned and gasped. Tim Wagner—Caedes the Destroyer—looked back at me. I gripped my wand and aimed it at him.

Tim raised his hand. "I'm not here to hurt you. I'm here to help."

I frowned. "You expect me to believe that?"

"My sacrifice did more than save my grandson," Gerhard explained. "When Hana sent my son to me, when we were reunited, it also purged him of his darkness."

"How can you be free of dark power when you literally exist in the arcane wells? It's all around you."

"What is light or dark in a realm with no natural source of light?" Tim asked. "It's not a matter of different kinds. Arcane power is arcane power. What separates a mage like you from the kind I became in my life is moderation. The darker parts of the wells are only darker because the arcane energies there are more concentrated. Once a mage taps into that kind of intense power, it's addictive."

Gerhard put his hand on his son's shoulder. "Absolute power corrupts absolutely. What my sacrifice did for Tim is what it did for Hans. It showed him that freedom comes more through weakness than strength. We need not gain more power to find peace. Quite the contrary, the more power we claim, the more we're pressured to use it, to rely on it, to make choices that alter the course of others' lives. Even the world."

I held Wand in my hand and examined it. "What is the difference between arcane power and this energy enchanted in my wand? What happened to you when I hit you with it?"

Gerhard grinned. "It changed my color."

"Mine, too." Tim winked. "Despite what Kermit used to say, being green isn't so bad."

I rubbed my brow. "I'm sorry. Hearing you tell jokes is a bit surreal."

"You're more accustomed to a murderous Caedes," Tim acknowledged. "I get it. Your power isn't unwelcome. It didn't change us. It is nostalgic. It reminds us of the beauty of the earth, of the world above, of everything I took for granted before."

"I don't understand. I put you in a prison for twenty years. You fed on dark power all that time. You murdered people. You killed the mother of your son and then you murdered more to plunge yourself deeper into the wells, to acquire the strength to raise her from the dead. Then, once you did it, she killed you."

Tim nodded. "I deserved it."

"You're not resentful?"

"Why would I be?"

"Maybe because you were never happy in life. You became a monster in an ass-backward attempt to correct a mistake, to bring back the woman you killed. Now you're dead. That sounds like a recipe for eternal torment if there is any such thing. If not due to the guilt you *should* feel for all you've done, then justice demands it."

"What is justice?" Gerhard asked. "On Earth, it seems, we think justice is primarily punitive. We think it means getting what one deserves. That's not accurate. Justice is primarily about setting things right and putting things into balance. True justice is not merely punitive, it's restorative."

"I've suffered for my deeds," Tim added. "While it might not seem like it's been very long since I died, since Hana snuffed out my life and stole my power in the park, time works differently here. I've been punished. I've also been restored."

"I don't understand," I pressed. "Hana was dead a lot longer, but she came back corrupted."

"Restoration cannot be forced on anyone," Gerhard explained patiently. "Those who insist on embracing their darkness will wallow in it. Those who refuse to find peace can never find it. What is not broken cannot be fixed. No one can win a battle if he does not confront his true enemy."

"The enemy wasn't *you*," Tim said. "It never was. I was always my own worst enemy. I never saw it in life. I wish I had and could have made better choices. Still, I lived my life. I died at the proper time. I have no desire to return from the grave, because it's here where I found peace."

I pressed my lips together. "All right. Well, I have to get out of here."

Gerhard shook his head. "No. You have to stop Hana. We're going to help you do that."

"How? What can we do from within here?"

"Cut her off," Tim replied. "That magic you blasted us with will seal the fissures from the inside out. We'll have to fight past all the other restless dead who Hana recruited first, but we can do it."

I looked around. There were still several other spirits surrounding us. "These other ghosts will help us do it?"

Gerhard nodded. "There's one thing you should know. You might not like it."

"What's that?"

"If we do this, it will stop Hana. Any she's raised will either immediately return to this dimension or wander the world as restless spirits. Such spirits aren't harmless, but without arcane power, they won't be able to do any real damage. There's just one other complication you must consider."

"I'm listening."

"That magic you're wielding may seal off the arcane wells for good."

"For good? Are you saying I won't be able to cast magic anymore?"

Gerhard nodded. "I'm saying *no one* will access the arcane wells again."

"How can I make that decision for everyone? It's not my place."

"Because if you don't, Hana will succeed," Tim said. "She's released too much energy into the world as it is. If you don't end it now, our worlds will merge. The dead will torment the living. The power here will remake the world you know into something else, something none of us can possibly predict."

"Will it be permanent?" I asked.

Gerhard shook his head. "There's no way to know for sure. Perhaps, in time, you'll find a way to access the wells again. You must face the very real possibility, however, that once this is done, it might *really* be done."

I looked at Wand. Letting go of magic forever was a big ask, but it wasn't a difficult decision. Not compared to the alternative. We had reason to believe that Hana had resurrected Hitler, of all people. Doing this would end him and anyone else she brought back through necromancy. She was in a position to wipe out our entire alliance now that she'd silenced their magic. What would happen to my family if I didn't do this? Would I make it back to them alive?

"If that's what has to be done, let's do it."

"There's also only one way back," Tim warned me. "Once you seal the fissures, it's the only thing left that will connect this realm to your world."

I sighed. "The portal that brought me here. If I go back through that gate, I'll be in the sky above the city, falling to a certain death."

"You could escape through a fissure direction," Gerhard suggested. "But you wouldn't return to your physical body. You'd return as a wandering and restless spirit."

"You don't want that," Tim added. "I was restless while still alive. Being at rest is far better. Any spirit here can testify to that truth."

I didn't want to die. I wanted to get back to my family. That was all I could think about. *My family.* Maybe I'd fall to the ground and survive by a miracle. I'd heard stories about skydivers who happened to survive after their chutes didn't open. I doubted they lived *well* after that. Hard to enjoy life after breaking every bone in your body. I had to make a choice. My life, or my family.

It wasn't a choice at all.

CHAPTER TWENTY-NINE

It was one thing to fight a battle between mages, even those raised by necromancy, on Earth. Fighting a war between spirits, in an ethereal plane of existence, was something else entirely. It was more than a fight between good and evil. It was a battle for peace, between those who wanted to preserve their peace and those who were restless. Between those who wanted to maintain peace for both the living and the dead and those who thought they'd find peace by destroying it for everyone, by spreading their restlessness like a contagion from their graves into the living world.

It was strange to find myself on the same side as my former nemesis. I suppose I always figured that if someone was a piece of crap in life, they'd stay that way for all eternity, however the afterlife looked. Once a douche, always a douche. Put it on a t-shirt.

Nothing about the ethereal realm was like I'd expected before I'd gone there. There wasn't a clear divide between good and bad magic, between the blue arcane power I wielded and the dark violet power that Hana and Caedes used before. Shades and concentrations of the power didn't infect someone because of the magic's type but affected someone because of the disposition of the mage himself. The restless spirits took in more power, like an addict who thought the answer was always more, never less. Arcane mages exercised restraint. We took in the power we could handle before the quantities we absorbed constitutionally altered our souls. You might say it was like a lot of drugs. The right dosage has benefits that outweigh the side effects. Take too much? The side effect they always gloss over with super-fast verbiage on the commercials, like "possibly even death," becomes more likely with excessive dosages. Arcane magic was like that. My son was able to tap into the dark, concentrated power that leaked through the fissures because he didn't have a wand that filtered the power and focused it. His spirit was open, innocent, and curious. As a mage he was raw, and he could wield raw power. It was risky. I could only pray to a god I wasn't sure I believed in that it didn't change him in any way.

I followed Gerhard and Tim through a void. They seemed to know where they were going, though I wasn't sure how it was possible to navigate in a world where everything looked the same and the arcane magic that swirled in the air was constantly moving and changing and flowing in various directions. When I'd been there before, the magic had flowed toward the fissure. With a spiderweb of cracks bursting into the material world, the flow of magic was moving in many directions all at once.

I wasn't looking forward to this, but I had to seal off the fissures. I'd get back to Elijah's portal and hope by a wing and a prayer I'd find just enough magic left to attempt an arcane barrier before whatever power lingered in the air or in my body was gone for good.

A barrier like that might not work. When I was in school, we had a competition to see who could create something that would protect an egg when we dropped it from the roof. I tried a barrier then and my egg was still scrambled before it hit the ground. I needed a parachute. Unfortunately, they don't manufacture those in the ethereal realm.

I tried not to think about it. Save my family, first. Save the world while I'm at it. If I couldn't save myself, it would suck ass. I wouldn't go to my death joyfully, singing hymns of praise to whoever might be listening. I'd probably fall to the Earth extending my middle finger to whoever might be the author of destiny. That didn't mean I wouldn't do it. My life for my family? There was no debate, but it was still scary as hell. I did my best not to think about it. One impossibility at a time was all I could wrap my mind around.

I don't know how long we walked. Like Tim and Gerhard said, time was different there, but I still experienced time relative to my own successive thoughts. It felt like we'd been walking for days. Was time passing on in the physical world at a similar rate? When I went to the ethereal realm before, only a few seconds had passed on Earth relative to what felt like hours in the ethereal realm. I was holding out a little hope. Hans couldn't cast, but he and Evander could help Elijah, and they might be able to figure out how to catch me in another portal and drop me closer to the ground. It was a small miracle that Elijah had managed to cast the first portal, though. What were the chances he'd do it again, and connect his gate to a location that would offer me a softer, less deadly, landing?

Eventually, I saw several violet blasts heading upward from a distance. As we got closer, I could see the spiderwebbed cracks meet at the location.

"That must be the army?" I asked.

Tim nodded. "If you want to call a host of restless and angry spirits harnessed by Hana's necromantic powers an army. It's more like a mob."

I glanced back at the group of spirits behind us. "Think we can take them?"

Gerhard shrugged. "We'll see. Keep in mind, however, that you cannot kill the dead."

I snorted. "Makes sense. What about me? I'm not technically dead. Not entirely, anyway. I still have a body I'd like to get back. Even if only for a few seconds while I fall to my likely death."

"Your body could be killed here," Gerhard pointed out. "You must be careful."

"If we can't kill the enemy, what happens when we fight?"

"Think of it more like a wrestling match. The goal is simply to overpower the other, to displace their position so you can get a clear shot at the fissure."

"If I do that, it will force Hana and her other armies back into this dimension?"

"It should," Gerhard agreed. "You may not have long after that happens to get back to your son's portal."

"It feels like we've been walking a long time."

"Trust your wand," Gerhard encouraged. "Allow it to take you to the portal."

"It will feel a lot faster that way," Tim added.

"Then why didn't we travel that way to get here?"

Tim laughed. "I said it would *feel* faster, not that it would *be* faster. Remember, time isn't really a thing here. What you experience as time, one moment to the next, is your mind trying to process all these events at once."

"Does that mean we've already won the battle?"

Tim gave me a sidelong glance. "It could just as easily mean you've already lost it. But you haven't won or lost it yet. Even though it's happening right now. Because there is now already, yet, or now. Actually, there's only and always now."

"My head hurts right now."

"Too bad there isn't a later for it to hurt less, unless of course, now has already passed into a new now when you've realized that your headache is just an illusion."

I grunted. "You get what I'm saying. All of this temporal nonsense is too much to wrap my mind around."

Gerhard smirked at me over his shoulder. "Which is exactly why you're experiencing your time here as a sequence of events rather than a cohesive, coherent, whole."

"You don't see it that way?" I asked.

"We've had time to adjust," Gerhard reminded me.

"So why don't you tell me? Is all of this going to work? What happens next?"

Tim snickered. "There is no next."

"For Pete's sake! Let's just do this."

CHAPTER THIRTY

Tim and Gerhard waved at the army of spirits that was following us through the ether, and they moved around us.

"What is going on?" I asked. "This isn't a battle formation."

"Does that enchantment in your wand also use your power?" Gerhard asked.

"I believe it does."

"We're going to pool our power and lend it to you. We'll keep the restless dead off of you, but it will surely take more than one blast from your wand to heal the fissure. Unless your blast is a lot stronger. Like I said before, you can't kill the dead. Once the fissure is healed, though, they'll have no reason to keep fighting. We just have to make sure you have one good shot and that it's strong enough to do the job."

"Who is going to clear the path?"

Gerhard laughed. "This is the realm of the dead, Thomas. We aren't the only ones with a vested interest in protecting the integrity of our rest."

I followed Gerhard's gaze back toward the direction we'd come from. More spirits were moving toward us, aglow with blue arcane energy. "This might just work."

Tim slapped me on the back. "By the way, old friend. I owe you an apology."

"You murdered people, Tim. An apology won't cut it."

"Fair enough. But it still needs to be said. I didn't see things the way I do now. I was obsessed with power. It consumed every cell of my body."

"I'm sorry as well."

"For what?" Tim asked.

"Burying you. Leaving you there, languishing underground in an arcane prison."

Tim shook his head. "Twenty years. It felt like a thousand. But I wasn't alone. Once I reached deeper into the wells, the spirits here were with me. The spirits of the dead, the restless. They weren't ideal company, but over time, I grew to be more like them. It wasn't until my father sacrificed himself, when he loosened the grip of the dark magic on my spirit and Hana took it for herself, that I realized the gravity of everything I'd done."

"Perhaps this will be for the best," I mused. "So long as there are mages in the world who can access the realms, there will be those tempted to the darkness, tempted to acquire more and more power. The only way to ensure there's never another Arcane War is to cut all of us off from the source."

"You won't be popular. There will be mages, devoid of power, who will blame you for it."

I chuckled. "As tempted as you were in those days by power, I was tempted by fame. I craved recognition and praise. I didn't just want to be the hero. I wanted the world to know I was the hero."

"We were all fools," Tim agreed. "We were young. That's the irony of youth, isn't it? No one thinks they're wiser than the young. Only those who realize they're fools are truly wise."

I chuckled. "That's profound. I'm impressed."

"I had a lot of time to think about it."

I cleared my throat. "Right. Twenty years."

He laughed. "Not in the prison. Here, in this place. Perhaps if there's any chance you can get back home and survive, you'll be able to benefit from the lesson in ways I never could."

I pressed my lips together. "I can't say I forgive you for what you did. It's not my place. But helping us end all of this is a start toward redemption."

Tim nodded. "Join the circle, Tom. We'll move in as soon as the other spirits give us a window."

I shoved Wand into my pocket and held out my hands. Tim took one, and Gerhard took the other. The other spirits joined to form a circle like the one we'd used back at headquarters to power our empaths. This time, though, I was the one harnessing their power. The energy would cycle through the circle. When the time was right, I'd grab my wand and blast the heart of the fissure.

The other spirits moved together like a raging river and charged the restless ghosts who were blasting their energy toward the fissure. Still holding hands, our circle moved in their wake, closer and closer to ground zero, the origin point from which all the cracks between the realms spread across St. Louis.

The power coursing through the circle was unlike anything I'd ever felt. Not different in kind so much as in potency. These mages were ethereal beings, inhabitants of the ethereal realm. Arcane magic was to them what oxygen was to me in the physical realm.

I saw the tip of my wand glowing from within my pocket. It was still green. The magic flowing from the circle powered it, and the enchantment converted that energy to the nature-based magic that Irene wielded and had evoked in her spell. It was ironic that we were now in the ethereal realm and Earth magic was the foreign power. Not that I'd had much experience with Earth magic, but it was very different to draw power from the world, from within one's own dimension. In its proper realm, each respective power had a home-field advantage. It was stronger. That's why Irene's magic was able to purge the dark arcane power from Berlin.

If I were fighting these restless mages, maybe I wouldn't be able to stop them. Not on their turf. Not with earthen magic. What I was about to do was more like giving the Earth itself a double-front attack on the invading powers.

When our circle reached a spot just under the fissure, the place where all the restless spirits were focusing their dark power before, I released Gerhard's hand and grabbed my wand.

I aimed at the fissure and blasted it with a stream of green energy. The earthen power wasn't precise. It didn't flow in a straight line from wand to target. It moved more like a river as it curled and wound its way to the fissure. It was wild—just like nature. The power from the other mages flowed through me like a conduit, and Wand converted the power and released it into the fissure.

I held the spell as long as I could until the power over-whelmed the center of the fissure and started to spread across the spiderweb of cracks that flowed from it. There wasn't exactly a ceiling in the ethereal realm. The cracks were spread across the ground in St. Louis, but here they shot out from the central fissure in every direction.

"Quick!" Gerhard shouted. "It's healing the fissure. You have to get back to your gate before it closes."

I didn't even have to direct Wand to do it. He had a person-ality of his own, and in this realm, he felt right at home. The next thing I knew, Wand was pulling me through the ethereal air. Gerhard, Tim, and the others disappeared in a matter of seconds. We were moving fast, but there was no wind, no reference point to judge how quickly Wand was pulling me through the realm.

Elijah's portal was still standing not far ahead. I had to reach it and hope it wouldn't spit me out in the skies over St. Louis. A skilled gate mage could move a portal even after it was cast, but Elijah didn't have a wand, and he only had a little training. Still, he had Hans and Evander. If they understood what happened, they might have moved the portal so I could come back through it safely.

I was like a heat-seeking missile, and the portal was my target. Wand was my navigation system.

I was getting close when several dark figures emerged at the event horizon of the portal. Hana landed in front of it with Goebbels behind her, and a dozen more mages followed.

Hana waved her hand through the air, and Elijah's portal disappeared.

"No!" I screamed as I reached Hana.

She had one hand on the hilt of her enchanted blade, and she laughed in my face. "Once again, Tommy, I have to admit that I underestimated you. You *almost* beat me. Your son, too. So much potential!"

"What did you do to him!"

"Calm down, Tommy. I didn't harm him or any of your friends. I simply cast a portal of my own and dropped us into your son's. I didn't have a choice. The fissures were healing. It was the last thing I could do before I got pulled back into this realm without my blade. Now all I have to do is use it again and I'll reopen the fissure."

"I'll stop you again!" I shouted.

"Not without your wand, you won't."

"I'm not giving it to you."

"And I'm not giving you this blade. If you want it, you'll have to take it from me."

I narrowed my eyes and gripped my wand with both hands to form a saber. "This is what it comes down to, then. You and me. If I win, I can use your blade to get home and close the fissure, earth-side. If you win, you take my wand and I'll be stuck here, powerless to stop you."

"Sounds about right. Don't think that I'm above playing dirty, though. I have an army at my side. Where is yours?"

I looked back over my shoulder. "They're coming. I think."

Hana raised her wand and formed a dark violet saber of her own. Her enchanted blade remained sheathed at her side. "It doesn't have to be this way, Tommy. If we fight, you'll lose. I'll kill your earthly body. You'll become a spirit like the rest of us. My offer stands. Join me, and I'll send you back to Earth in the flesh. Once I reopen the fissure, I'll take your wand, of course, but you can return to your family. You can enjoy the new world I'm making. A world where death is only temporary, where we all have a chance to return with power."

I took two steps back, still gripping Wand with both hands. Hana had me outnumbered. Goebbels was probably reading my mind at that very second. The earthen magic still flowed through my wand. My saber was green, not blue like before. Now, though, I was on her turf. I was fighting with earthen magic in an arcane dimension. Even if it was a fair fight, one-on-one against Hana, I'd be at a disadvantage. I couldn't defeat her and a dozen more mages loyal to her cause.

I had faced a lot of fears as of late. My fear of heights was a big one. My family was always my true north. They gave me strength, even in the direst circumstances. There wasn't anything I wouldn't give up for them. I'd give my life. I'd even give up the world.

The world Hana wanted to make wasn't the paradise she wanted me to believe, though. It was a world where deadly arcane power would be the primary currency. It was a world ruled by the restless, where people would live their lives only to come back as angst-ridden ghosts, restless power-hungry spirits like Hana and the others.

That wasn't a world I wanted for my family. I'd do anything to save them, but joining Hana wasn't the answer.

I widened my stance and raised my saber. "I don't surrender for my family, Hana. I fight for them."

Hana sighed and shook her head. "It's your funeral. If that's your choice, so be it."

CHAPTER THIRTY-ONE

Hana charged at me with her saber, and I blocked her strike with mine. Nigel's training was paying off. I spun and took a swipe at her, but she blocked me easily.

She was good. She knew what she was doing. I put everything I had into each attempt to strike, but she was toying with me. Her other mages formed an arc around us, holding crooked wands with violent arcane energy illuminating the tips.

So long as she had the upper hand, I hoped they wouldn't blast me. The moment I started to win, though, they'd take me down. The cards were all stacked against me. I couldn't win.

Hana held her saber with one hand. She blocked another one of my strikes and with her opposite hand blasted me in the chest with dark magic. I felt the impact of the strike, and it thrust me violently through the air. I landed on my back on…something. There wasn't soil or dirt. Not even a visible surface. The force of my body striking it was enough to prove that there was a ground of some kind.

"I'm going to give you one more chance to surrender, Tommy. You can't beat me."

"Why do you want me to join you so badly? Why not just kill me and be done with it!"

Hana walked over to me as I struggled back to my feet. "I have my reasons."

"It's Hans, isn't it?"

"Why would he have anything to do with this?"

"You want me alive. He'll never join you if I don't first."

"I told you before. He doesn't matter. I will complete my plan with or without him."

"But he's still what makes you restless, isn't he? You might be content to remain a restless spirit on Earth, but there's more than one way to let go. You either find peace, or you lose all hope, you let go. If I'm not there, if you kill me, you're afraid he'll become a lost cause. You'll cease to be restless."

"It doesn't matter! I'm going to do this one way or another!"

"But you're afraid of finding peace, aren't you? You're so addicted to your angst, your vengeance, your restlessness, that you think you'll lose power if you ever let go."

"You're not his father. Your wife is not his mother. I am his mother!"

I nodded. "You admit it, then. You know he's found happiness with my family, and you're afraid if you destroy me, if I don't come back, you'll lose your opportunity to find peace by reconciling with him. You'll have no choice but to let go, to move on, to remain here even if the worlds are merged, because peaceful spirits don't return to Earth."

"You're clever, Tommy. When I'm done, though, all the spirits will be restless. There will be no peace."

"That's what the peaceful spirits here fear. That's not exactly true, though, is it?"

"If they fear losing their peace, that's enough to make them restless."

"You can't impose fear on someone, Hana. How someone handles their fear is their own choice. I won't lie to you. I'm terrified. I don't know if I'll ever get out of here. It's still my choice to give in to that fear and surrender, or to fight. Every spirit has that choice. You can't take that from them."

Behind me, someone said, "That's right."

Hana gasped. "Timothy?"

I spun to see Tim standing behind me with Gerhard. The rest of our army of mages approached at a distance.

Tim shook his head. "You can't do this, Hana. I raised you because I wanted to be together. I wanted to be a family. I underestimated how much the dark power corrupted you."

"It corrupted you first!"

Tim shook his head. "Even so, despite all the travesties I committed, I did everything because there was something human that remained. I wanted to fix my mistake, to have a family, even if I had to do unspeakable things to make it so. Tommy was a better man than I ever was. He stood and fought for his family, but he didn't run to darkness to do it. He still won't. And we won't let you force it upon him."

I nodded at Tim. He briefly made eye contact with me and nodded back.

"Your army is impressive," Hana admitted. "But there are more restless spirits here, ready to fight at my side."

"Then we fight," Tim said simply. "A final Arcane War, fought here, in the arcane dimension."

"That's ridiculous!" Hana shouted. "We can fight for all eternity here. We can't kill each other. We're already dead."

"That's right," Tim agreed. "We have nothing to lose. But you do. We'll fight until Tommy wrests that enchanted blade from your side."

"Not if I kill him first!" she screamed.

Hana gripped her wand with both hands, her violet saber still aimed at me, and charged. I blocked her, but it didn't matter. A dozen other mages stood behind her with wands pointed straight at me.

I raised an arcane barrier. It was green like all my other spells produced in conjunction with Irene's enchantment.

I swiftly darted out of the way of the first few missiles they fired at me, and Gerhard and the other mages swarmed around me. More dark figures, some illuminated by violet auras and others blue, swarmed around us from every direction. They all collided in blasts of arcane power.

Hana sprung to her feet and I braced myself to clash sabers. She formed a gate between us and took one shot. It bounced off my barrier. She jumped into the air and fired again, and this time she struck Gerhard in the chest before she jumped into her portal.

"Damn it!" I shouted.

"He'll be fine," Tim assured me. "He'll be stunned for a minute or so, but that's the most that can happen to us here."

"Where did she go?" I asked.

"She's here. She can't gate directly out of the arcane dimension. Not unless she uses that enchanted sword again."

"She doesn't need to," I reminded him. "All she has to do is get away from us so she can use the blade."

"But you could just seal it all over again."

I nodded. "That's right. And if I do that while she's on Earth, she'll be forced back here without the blade. You can't take your toys with you when you die."

Hans twirled his wand in his hand. "Not most of them, anyway."

I silently nodded in agreement. A mage's wand was the one thing we could take with us in death, and that was because the wand was connected to a mage's spirit and empowered by an ethereal spirit. "She's bluffing. She won't leave without making sure I'm done first. Otherwise I could seal her fissure again and bring her back here without the blade."

"But you'd also be stuck here. You couldn't get back to your family without the blade. Perhaps she's calling your bluff."

Tim and I each had arcane barriers around us, but they wouldn't hold for long. "We need to go after her," I decided. "One way or another, every spirit in this realm can fight forever, but the only way either side wins is if Hana gets my wand or I take her sword."

Tim nodded. "Use your wand to fly. Go after her. I'll stay behind you to watch your six."

I nodded and squeezed Tim's shoulder. I never once thought in a million years I'd be trusting Tim, Caedes the Destroyer, my onetime mortal enemy, to watch my back.

I dispelled the saber and raised Wand into the air. He pulled me from the ground, and I didn't need to tell him where to go. We were of one mind—in an almost literal sense. Tim flew behind me as blue and violet spirits collided around us, tossing blasts of energy all around.

What would happen if Hana made the fissure and went through it? If I went with her and sealed the fissure from the other side, I'd be able to kill her and she couldn't take the sword with her. It would fall to the ground. I also wasn't sure what would happen if I went through the fissure. Before, when I entered the ethereal realm, I had to go back to a gate and use it to reforge my material body on Earth. Going straight through a fissure made me more like a ghost than a living man. Hana pulled it off, though. When she used that blade, with whatever enchanted energy was within it, the body she emerged with was as good as her original body. I wasn't all that well versed in the mechanics of gate magery. If I found Elijah, since his gate was what sent me into the ethereal realm, he *might* be able to cast another gate over me to restore my natural body.

Hana must've known that if she returned and I followed her, it would make her more vulnerable. She also knew that fighting me here, as the spirits closed in around us, was risky. We were each as likely to be struck by another spirit as we were each other. Given how much better she was with her blade when we had fought before, perhaps she wanted to lure me away where the odds were less evenly split, where she'd be able to take me on where she had an advantage.

There was more than one way for mages to do battle, and she wasn't a natural battlemage. The only reason she could make a saber at all was because she'd taken power that wasn't naturally hers into herself from the darker wells. I should be able to hold my own in a straight-up battle. She might know how to wield a sword, and could use that against me, but whatever battlemagery she used wasn't as pure or as powerful as mine. It wasn't even as pure as Tim's natural-born battle magic.

I had an idea. It was a huge risk but it might work. The only question was would Hana buy it?

I glanced at Tim as he flew beside me. "If I raise my fist in the air, take a shot at her."

Tim gave a firm nod of approval. "She's fast. I don't know if I can. If she flies through another gate before I can hit her…"

"Be ready. I have an idea. It's risky and probably won't work, but it's also the best shot we've got."

"What's the idea?" Tim asked.

I shook my head. "Never know when Goebbels is listening, or if he can communicate back to Hana. You'll have to trust me on this."

"All right, old friend. I'll do whatever I can."

Gate magery wasn't as handy in the ethereal realm as it was back on Earth. Here, with Wand, I could fly almost anywhere. I just had to know where to go. The length of a journey one had to take was more a product of the mind than the laws of physics. Newton didn't have a damn thing to say about arcane physics. Einstein might have known better. Whatever the case, with focus and intention, I could fly to wherever Hana went through a portal and I wouldn't be far behind.

It was all starting to make sense. Before, when I first arrived in the ethereal realm, I was afraid to get too far from the gate home. I was anxious about the fissure and what was ahead, so the journey matched the condition of my mind. My apprehension made the journey long. My angst turned it arduous. Now I was determined, and I had a plan.

It was either the dumbest idea I'd ever had or the smartest. I'd find out which one it was soon enough.

It wasn't long before we saw Hana in the distance, blasting in her violet energies with her enchanted sword in one hand and her wand in the other.

We flew near her and I put Wand back in my pocket and raised my hands. "You win. I get it. I can't stop you."

Tim gasped. "Tom! You can't—"

I raised my hand to silence him. "I just want to see my family again."

"You know the price," Hana reminded me. "You won't be powerless without it, but I'm afraid I can't have you mangling up all my efforts."

I nodded. "I understand. I'll give it to you once you open the fissure again."

"You don't trust me, Tommy? I'm offended!"

Tim grunted. "Do you blame him? I brought you back from the dead and you turned on me not a minute later."

Hana shrugged. "It was only temporary, dear. If you knew my plans, you'd realize as much."

I shook my head. "Your plans changed. This wasn't what you tried to do first when you attacked the Entente alliance."

Hana shrugged. "I needed to tie up a few loose ends first. That's all that was."

I sighed. "It doesn't matter anymore."

She unsheathed her sword. This was the only chance I might get. I had to act while she was cutting open the fissure. I reached into my opposite pocket and pulled out the small pouch that held the enchanted pendant Irene gave me. It wouldn't silence Wand. It would silence whatever mage held it or wore it. Careful not to touch it myself, I stuck the tip of Wand into the pouch while Hana was slicing her enchanted blade through the ethereal dimension.

Hold on to it, Wand. Don't let it loose. Take it to her.

Wand pulsed in my hand, confirming he'd understood my thoughts.

"Hand it over," Hana snapped. "You're free to leave."

"I still won't have a normal body, will I?"

"What is a normal body? You'll be like me. You'll see your family and they'll see you. Surely that's sufficient."

I shook my head. "I'll be like you. Connected to the ethereal realm. So long as I remain restless and not at peace."

"If seeing your family puts you at peace, well, that's your problem. Surely, given all your pride, all your aspirations, there's a lot more that you'll regret. More to keep you restless and alive."

I held out Wand. The magic within my wand bound itself to the pendant. Perhaps it was the similar enchantments, drawing them to one another like a magnet to metal. Or maybe it was Wand, responding to my thoughts before. Either way, it was subtle enough that Hana wouldn't notice until it was too late.

I released Wand and he went flying to Hana. She caught him. When she did, the pendant slipped down Wand and onto her wrist.

Hana gasped. For a moment, she was powerless.

I raised my fist into the air.

Tim blasted her in the chest with an arcane missile.

The force of the blast sent her flying into the fissure.

"Go after her!" Tim shouted.

I dove with all my strength into the fissure. Without Wand to pull me toward it, even if I wasn't in my actual body, my legs responded as any forty-two-year-old's might. They ached as I leaped.

I wasn't sure whether this would work or not. I wouldn't know until I arrived back on Earth.

I shot out of the fissure with more force than I'd anticipated. I'd like to say I landed gracefully on my feet, but I was no acrobat. If it wasn't for the pea gravel in the playground at Gregory Park I might have hurt myself. I landed on my back, which gave me the perfect angle to see Hana on the merry-go-round and the force of magic spewing from Wand sending them spinning as Hana tried to pry her fingers off my wand.

I managed to get to my feet. "That enchantment is in my wand. It sets all things right as they should be. You can't fight like a battlemage now. All you have is your portal magic, and it looks like you can't even use that, since, you know… You shouldn't be here."

Hana screamed. "This won't work! I'll just come back again!"

I laughed and stopped the merry-go-round. Hana had already re-sheathed her enchanted blade and was stuck fighting with Wand. I took her sword from her.

"Will you now?"

Hana shrieked. "You son of a bitch!"

I shook my head. "Hana, Hana, Hana. Why bring my mother into this? Wand, time to finish this."

Wand flexed and bent until it pointed straight at Hana. It unleashed its magic on her, enveloping her in green, snuffing out the little bit of violet dark magic that remained within her. Her body turned into green energy infused by Wand's enchantment, and the fissure sucked her into it like a Cheerio into a vacuum hose.

The energy in Hana's body also healed the fissure. Wand remained where the fissure used to be in a pile of pea gravel, and I reached into the gravel and pulled it out. There was still a little magic within it, something left over from the enchantment.

The moment I grabbed him, the rest of Wand's magic flowed up my arm and through my body. He was fixing me, changing me, making me the way I was supposed to be. He was setting things right.

The sensation almost tickled, sort of like when the feeling comes back to your leg after you'd been sitting on the toilet, probably on your phone, for a bit too long. Don't tell me that hasn't ever happened to you. We've all been there.

When my body returned to normal, Wand was cold in my hand. I didn't feel any power within him. I tried to cast a simple spell, an arcane barrier, but nothing happened. The only magic I had access to was in Hana's blade, the only thing I had that might reopen the arcane realm to us again. Provided, of course, that it would work from this side of the old fissure as well as from within the ethereal dimension.

I didn't have a phone on me. If I really had cut off the arcane wells from all the mages, Jessie wouldn't sense that I was back, and Hans couldn't pick me up. I had no choice but to walk.

I straightened out my shirt and sat on one of the park benches to shake the pebbles from my shoe. Then someone touched my shoulder. I turned and gasped.

"Tim? How the hell did you get back here?"

Tim shook his head. "I don't know. I hit Hana with an arcane missile. When she returned through the portal, the magic that sent her back sucked me right out again. It took a minute, but before the magic faded, I got my body back again."

I shook my head. "This isn't going to be easy, Tim. People here know you as Caedes the Destroyer."

"Caedes is dead. I left him behind in the wells. Do you think Hans would be open to seeing me?"

I pressed my lips together. "I suppose we can find out. Follow me. We have a long walk ahead."

CHAPTER THIRTY-TWO

It was a long and awkward walk back to the alliance headquarters. Unfortunately, I hadn't driven when I went there before. My phone still didn't work, but someone there would have one so I could call Kat to pick us up.

It was strange seeing Tim Wagner, Caedes the Ex-Destroyer, walking beside me, in a black robe of all things. There are a lot of Catholics in St. Louis. Perhaps people would think he was a friar or something.

"What am I going to do?" Tim asked. "I didn't ask to come back, but now that I'm here, I have to figure this out."

I sighed and shook my head. "We'll talk to Nigel. He has some connections. We might be able to get you a new identity. Still, the mages here in St. Louis will recognize you. There's no avoiding that."

"I don't feel any magic at all. We aren't mages anymore, Tom."

I heaved a deep, heavy sigh. "I don't know. Maybe it's temporary. Maybe it will come back. Either way, magic or not, people will remember the things you did before. I don't know that there's much of anything you can do to make up for that. Some things don't balance on the scales of justice. You can't bring back people who died."

"Actually…"

"You know what I mean. Even if we could do it, we can't do it now. Not without using this blade, and that would be too risky."

Tim nodded. "It's all right. I'm at peace with the mages I killed as Caedes. Most of them have no more desire to return than I did. Making peace with their families is another matter."

"Like I said, a new identity might be helpful. Leaving town would probably be in your best interest as well."

"What about Hans?" Tim asked.

I shrugged. "I can't tell you how he feels or if he'll be open to it. He doesn't remember much about who you used to be, only what he's heard."

"He remembers what I did before. When I tried to kill you. He saved your life."

I chuckled. "Yeah. Good times."

"What are you going to do next? Now that we can't access the arcane wells, I suppose you'll have to find something to keep yourself occupied."

I laughed. "You're kidding, right? I have a business that I've been neglecting ever since I inherited it from my father-in-law. I have three boys who are a handful. I have a bunch of British mages, or ex-mages, who are looking to me for guidance. I suppose a few of them might want jobs, but I can't hire them all."

"At least you have skills. What in the world am I going to do? The only thing I've ever been good at is homicide, and that's not what most people would consider a marketable skill."

I stopped at a crosswalk and pressed the "walk" button. "I guess you'll have to pick up where you left off when we were teenagers. Time to figure out what you're good at, what you like to do."

Tim shook his head. "That won't be easy. My family always

had money, but that's not mine. I'm sure Hans inherited most of it."

"He handles most of the family accounts. Technically, the bulk of it remains in Rose's name."

Tim's lip quivered. "My mom… How is she?"

I shrugged. "Dementia has taken its toll, but she's been doing better. It's hard to know how well she'll do without her abilities as an empath. All the voices she heard before were confusing, but she's learned to adapt to it with the help of other empaths."

"I imagine change of any sort is difficult for her."

I nodded. "It is. But I know she'll be happy to see you. If there's anyone who never lost hope in you it was her."

Tim huffed. "Probably because she couldn't remember the worst of what I'd done."

"Maybe, maybe not. Still, she's a mother. You're a father. While you're still getting used to that, trust me when I say that there's nothing that compares to a parent's love for a child. She may or may not remember Caedes the Destroyer. She certainly remembers Timmy Wagner."

Tim cleared his throat. "It's Tim, Tommy."

I laughed. "And it's Tom, Timmy. We aren't kids anymore. But your mother will still see you that way. It doesn't matter how old you get. To our mothers, we're always their babies."

Someone had taped over a few fingers on the "don't walk" sign so that when it lit up it looked like the red hand was flipping us off. Eventually it changed to the glowing blue walking man who looked a lot like an arcane mage back in the ethereal realm. We crossed the street. We still had several blocks to go.

"Do you think they'll throw me in jail?"

I shook my head. "I don't know, Tim. Most everyone thinks you're dead. If I were you, I'd keep a low profile. See your son and your mother, but no one else needs to know you're here. Not until you can start a new life with a new identity."

"If they threw me in jail, I'd deserve it."

I nodded. "I don't think that Wand brought you back just so you could rot in a cell. You're here for a reason. Maybe it's something simple, a chance to get to know your son."

"Sounds complicated."

I smiled. "You're probably right. It won't be easy. Still, perhaps there's another reason you're back. The witch who enchanted my wand said that the magic was supposed to set things right. For whatever reason, you being alive must be a part of that."

"Those people still deserve justice."

I snorted. "You did twenty years. You didn't even get a jury to deliberate your case. I was the judge and jury."

"Doesn't matter. You were right to do what you did."

"Still, you served your time. You also got the death penalty. Being back again, for whatever reason that might be, is a clean slate so far as I'm concerned. I wouldn't be here without you. Our world wouldn't be the same if you didn't step up and fight. Like I told you before, back in the arcane dimension, it's a start on the path toward redemption. What you do next determines whether you'll stay on the path or not."

Tim shook his head. "I didn't deserve another chance at life."

"Sometimes it's not about what we deserve that matters. It's what we do with what we've been given, if we make the most of our opportunities, and don't take the important things for granted, that defines us. You aren't the same person you were before. You were enthralled by dark power."

"That's not an excuse. I still did the things I did."

"You're right. It's not an excuse. But the very fact that you realize that means you aren't beyond redemption. Don't forget your past. Don't live in it, either. All we have is now."

Tim tilted his head. "Are you sure we aren't still in the arcane dimension?"

I smiled. "Maybe the two worlds aren't as different as they seem. It's all a matter of perspective, I suppose. What might have happened in the past, or what could happen in the future, never matters as much as the present. I, for one, am going to remember that when we get back to the headquarters and I can hug my son, when I see my other boys and take them in my arms, and when I kiss Kat again. For too long, I allowed fear to motivate me, but when we're stuck in fear, it's always rooted in the past or the future. It stems from wounds we suffered before, or from worries about things that might never come to pass. If we're living in fear, if we're living in the past or the future, we're blind to the now. We miss out on life itself."

We finally made it back to the headquarters, and Tim decided to wait a block or so away. If we still had other American mages there, he was the last person any of them would want to see, especially now that everyone had lost their powers.

I imagined everyone was in a panic trying to figure out what happened. Would they be angry at me for it or grateful? It didn't matter. My family was safe. They were safe. If Hana had brought Hitler back from the dead, he was dead again as well. I'd done the best I could to save the world from a horror most of the mages waiting inside couldn't even fathom. That was enough for me. Doing the right thing isn't about recognition, or praise, or fame, or making an extra buck.

I knew in my heart that no matter what anyone else thought, I'd done the best I could. I was satisfied with that.

I pressed open the front doors. I walked down the hallway and made my way to the cafeteria.

"Daddy!" Elijah shouted as he ran into my arms. "I thought I killed you!"

Tears were flowing down his face. Jessie and Hans were crying too but they gave us our space. "You didn't kill me. You saved me."

"What happened?" Nigel asked as he approached. "None of us can access the arcane wells."

I sighed. "Elijah's portal sent me into the arcane realm. It's a long story, but I was able to get the sword from Hana and seal the fissure. The only downside to all of that is that the magic I used, the stuff the witch gave me when she enchanted my wand, sealed off the arcane wells. We aren't mages anymore."

Nigel narrowed his eyes. "Are you sure about that?"

"What do you mean?" I asked.

Nigel cleared his throat. "Show your father, Elijah."

Elijah gave me a tight squeeze before releasing me from his embrace. He extended his hand and a green circle appeared in the middle of the room. A matching green portal showed up on the other side of the room. Elijah stepped through it and appeared at his other gate. He waved at me from a distance. I waved back. Then he stepped back through and released it.

"I don't understand. How did you do that?"

"All the children seem to have the ability to wield this new magic."

I scratched my head and pulled Wand from my pocket. The green glow that illuminated him before returned. I quickly formed a barrier—I'd call it an arcane shield, but I wasn't sure that what I was using was arcane. The new barrier had a green rather than blue glow.

"Holy sh—" I caught myself. Elijah was there. "Shazam. Holy shazam!"

"That's not what you were going to say, Dad."

I chuckled. "You're right. But it's what I should have said."

"Any thoughts on what's going on, Thomas?" Nigel asked.

I thought for a moment. "The fissures before are now sealed with earthen magic, the stuff that the witch in Germany used. A whole army of spirits channeled their power into me so I could seal the fissures from within the arcane dimension. That energy must be coursing through the old fissures now."

"Like ley lines," Nigel theorized. "Natural pathways of magic that druids and witches often use in their magic. It appears you've created a whole new network of ley lines. From what I can tell, the lines of magic spreading from here are expanding. We have to figure out how it works."

I twirled my wand in my hand. "Our wands were originally forged in the arcane realm. Perhaps we'll need a witch to turn our wands to these ley lines. Until then, it looks like we'll be taking classes from our children. They're the ones with all the power, now."

"Them and you," Nigel pointed out. "You might want to keep that to yourself. Most of the mages are asleep at the moment. If they learn that you cut them off, but still have power yourself, it may look suspicious."

I shrugged. "I understand. I have no need for magic. Not so long as there aren't any nasty mages out there with world-ending aspirations who need their butts kicked."

Nigel grinned. "For all our sakes, mate, I hope we don't see anyone like that for some time."

I bit my lip. "About that. I have an old friend who might need a favor. Before you freak out when I tell you who it is, I need you to promise to hear me out."

Nigel nodded. "Don't tell me you brought someone back with you from the other side."

I cleared my throat. "Hans, would you come over here for a moment?"

"Sure thing. What's up?"

"How'd you like to go outside and meet your father?"

"You're shitting me."

Elijah giggled. "How does someone even *do* that? Wouldn't it hurt real bad to poop out a whole person?"

Hans winced. "Sorry."

"It's all right. I almost let an s-bomb fly myself a few minutes ago. I'm serious, Hans. He's back. But he's not the man he became. He's more like the boy he used to be."

"Fascinating," Nigel put in. "A dark mage, purged of his darkness through death. How in the world did he get back?"

I shook my head. "I'm not sure. I think the magic in my wand pulled him out of there. He helped me defeat Hana. I think for the time being, though, it might be best if we keep his existence on the down low."

"I'd like to interview him, if that's all right," Nigel said.

"He'll need new identification," I suggested.

"That can be arranged. Still, I'd like to check him out and see if he is truly clean of dark power before we offer him any help at all."

"You're sure he wants to see me?" Hans asked.

"You and your grandmother. He is a bit nervous about it. He knows all he did before. He remembers it, but he isn't proud of any of it. He's not the same dark mage everyone knew as Caedes. He's Timmy Wagner, the friend I thought I'd lost decades ago."

Jessie stepped over. "Sorry, I was listening in."

"You can hear us?" I asked.

"Not as an empath, dumbass. With my ears. I can hear with those things too, you know."

I chuckled. "Right. Of course."

"Timmy's really back?"

I nodded. "He's waiting outside. He's afraid of what people will do if they see him. For good reason. I don't think most of the mages, especially the American mages, would understand."

"The American mages went home when the fissure closed," Jessie informed me. "Our gate mages couldn't do it, so it was Uber city here for a while."

"How long was I gone, exactly?" I asked. "It felt like several hours."

"The fissures healed almost the second you disappeared in Elijah's portal." Hans looked at his phone to check the time. "That was about six hours ago."

I pressed my lips together. "It took a lot longer in my recollection to heal the fissures than what happened after. Funny how time syncs up differently in the ethereal realm with our world."

"It's curious though," Nigel mused. "How long would you say it was from the time you arrived in the ethereal realm before you sealed the fissures?"

I shrugged. "I don't know. Half a day, at least."

"There must be something about that magic, the earthen magic, that set that realm into congruence with our world. After you healed the fissures, time there and here may have started to flow together."

"Does that mean we aren't entirely cut off from the arcane wells?"

"I'm not sure what it means," Nigel admitted. "Let's pay Timothy Wagner a visit. Perhaps he can shed some light on all of this. If he cannot, I'll return to Berlin myself. We need to find that witch."

CHAPTER THIRTY-THREE

The reunion between Tim and Hans and Rose went better than expected. Nigel was able to use his contacts with the British government to secure a new identity for Tim. He was now technically a citizen of England with a visa to the United States. It sufficed. For the time being, he was staying in the old Wagner house with Rose and Hans. He kept a low profile. The family had plenty of money, but without any world-saving endeavors to occupy our time, and very little we could do in the way of training at the headquarters, Hans was putting in a lot more time working for me at the rental store.

Nigel left the country a few days after we got back, and he went looking for Irene in hopes of discovering the truth about the power she'd infused in my wand. I could still cast pretty much everything I was able to do since Wand was enchanted. The only major difference so far as I could tell was that my magic had a different hue. What was blue before was now green. All my basic, universal, mage abilities were intact, too, which was odd considering that I was the only grown-up mage who wasn't totally silenced.

Classes still went on at the alliance headquarters. Professor

Poppycock—a.k.a. Pritchard, a.k.a. P-Dick—continued as he had before, lecturing on arcane theory, the history of magecraft, and the like. I attended all the classes along with Elijah who, suddenly, was the star of the show. His abilities were improving. While Evander and Hans couldn't cast gates themselves yet, they were able to give him a few pointers. Enough so that after a few weeks of practice he managed to form portals to and from our house and the alliance headquarters. Places he was familiar with, places that were along the cracks, the "ley lines," he could access with his gates. He was still a long way from being able to create gates that would send us to the other side of the planet. Still, progress was progress, and the young folk still needed mentoring, given the fact that they were the only ones who retained any ability to use magic. Anyone who'd had a wand, whose powers were tuned to the wells, was powerless. So, I didn't cast much. I didn't even carry Wand with me most of the time. Until we knew how we could help the other mages regain their abilities, it was best that way.

Apart from all of that, life got back to normal. Days passed, then weeks, and we still didn't have any definite updates from Nigel. I tried to check in every few days.

I got a new phone, always a momentous occasion. I was a bit peeved that the damn thing didn't even come with a charger. Just a cord that was supposed to plug into a USB block that didn't match any of the ones I had. What the hell, man? Next-day Prime delivery came to the rescue, and I could communicate with Nigel, who'd borrowed a phone before he left. If he found Irene or learned anything, he promised to let me know "straightaway." That's British for "immediately."

I started working full time at the store. Jeff had come a long way with his management skills. For the most part, he kept the show running. I focused more on paperwork, marketing, payroll, and all the bullshit that required coffee to complete. It wasn't so thrilling as battling undead mages or traversing other realms, but it paid the bills.

There was one major problem that required resolution. Domestic mages were totally helpless now that they didn't have their magic to cook and clean. The food at the alliance headquarters really went downhill. My father called us on a regular basis, begging us to go out to eat, so my mom wouldn't try to cook again. She nearly burned down the house trying to make a meatloaf.

He also wanted to know if I knew the names of any good housekeepers. As if I could ever afford one myself.

Kat found the whole thing humorous. All those years when my mother criticized Kat's ability to keep a clean house were coming home to roost.

That was the irony of the situation. Those mages whose skills were more useful on the regular found it a lot more difficult to adjust to magic-less life. Battlemages, though? Well, we hadn't had any reason to blow anything up in months. It wasn't much of an adjustment for us.

It was a relief. I still had my abilities, and if some kind of ethereal monster emerged from the depths of an unknown immortal realm, I'd be ready. Until then, though, it was all about spending as much time with my family as I could.

I might not have any need to defeat any real-life monsters, but when it came to playing with the boys, we always had monsters to fight. They were either made up entirely or manifested in the form of action figures.

Did you know they remade the Masters of the Universe action figures? When I discovered that, I bought each and every one for my boys. They didn't get it. I had to find the cartoons on a streaming service, and, how about that, they remade those, too. With my boys, we kicked Skeletor's bony ass nightly.

Life doesn't get much better than that.

Maybe I'd have to pick up my wand again. Perhaps some evil

lurked in the world, some insidious scheme that Irene planned from the start, or maybe the divide between our realm and the arcane dimension was temporary. It didn't matter. All I had was *now*. All that mattered was the present. Every moment I had with my boys, with my wife, even with my friends, Jessie, Hans, and yes, even Tim, was precious.

The other mages were waiting anxiously for news from Nigel, a way to get their powers back. I wasn't all that worried about it. In fact, secretly, a part of me hoped things would stay just as they were forever.

That wasn't life. Things would change, and when the future became the "now" I'd embrace that, too. For now, though, now was now—and I wouldn't change a thing.

APRIL 13, 2023

I have to confess—I'm a total nerd. I know this comes as a surprise. I mean, most fantasy authors are hip and cool, right? I'm totally the exception here, I get it.

We all have fantasies about having superpowers. Admit it. You've thought about it. I used to pray when I was a child that God would give me the powers of Superman. I even tried learning how to fly. I'd run and dive into the couch face-first. Each time I did it, I launched a little further from the couch than the time before. My reasoning? If I could add just an inch each time, with enough practice, I'd be able to fly!

Totally reasonable!

I also work out a lot. A part of the reason is because I harbor a secret fantasy of becoming a superhero. I must be strong if I'm going to defeat villains and save the world, right?

This fantasy was a way for me to indulge my superhero fantasies. Tom is a lot like me. He had three boys and, not coincidentally, I named them after my own. My middle name is "Thomas," and my father's middle name is "Gregory." My wife isn't a Kat—but she's been begging me to get a cat for months. It's only a matter of time before I give in and agree. I also said we wouldn't get another dog until the boys were grown and now we have two. The same goes for my oldest boy's hamster.

Tom Gregory has a lot of powers I'd like to have. His experience, though, is a lot like I'd expect if I had superpowers. Despite the thrilling adventures we see in comic books, there just isn't that much opportunity to fight villains and thwart world-threatening plots. Like Tom, I'd probably find myself with a lot of unusable powers, living a normal life, *waiting* for the opportunity to go to battle and defeat my imagined nemesis.

I'm not entirely sure at this point if I'm going to keep writing this series or if this is the end. You'll have to let me know what you think. Do you want more from our battlemage dad? How were the jokes? Were they five-groan worthy?

Whether we get more adventures with Tom or not, every story I write has a bit of my own personal superhero aspirations woven into it. I couldn't ever write normal thrillers or crime stories, or any other genre, that didn't involve magic. These books are fun to write because they allow me to entertain, even if only in my mind and through my keyboard, adventures I'll probably never have. Still, playing the hero from behind a computer screen is probably safer, so I suppose I'll count my blessings. Being an author probably allows for a longer life than being a superhero (unless I was invulnerable like Superman, of course) and I have three boys to raise. It doesn't get much better than that!

-Theo

APRIL 12, 2023

First, thank you for reading this story and these author notes in the back as well!

Caffeine, Jet Lag, and The Pinball of Life

As a frequent traveler, I'm no stranger to the challenges of jet lag. In my recent trip to Seville, Spain, I found myself turning to caffeine as a means to fight off the overwhelming urge to close my eyes and drift off to sleep while my brain refused to quiet down.

It's a battle many travelers can relate to, I'm sure.

Seville is a beautiful, historic city, but it also has its quirks. One is how sound travels in the narrow alleys near our Air-BnB.

Originally designed for horses and humans to navigate over 200 years ago, these alleys now serve as makeshift streets for modern cars with their stone and brick streets and stone walls.

The sounds of people talking and vehicles passing by reverberate off the stone walls, creating an interesting and rather loud white noise soundtrack for sleep.

These same alleys also present another challenge: incredibly narrow sidewalks, sometimes only 12 inches wide.

This means you're constantly dodging the occasional side

mirror or trying not to get clipped by a passing car. In short, it feels like you're the chrome ball in the great Pinball of Life game.

Despite the challenges, I'm appreciative of the chance to be here in Saville and speak with other Indie Authors at the 20Books Spain conference supported by Lantia!

Thank you for joining me on this journey, and I hope you continue to find excitement in the worlds I create.

Until the next adventure!

Ad Aeternitatem,

Michael Anderle

P.S.

The experience mentioned above is brought to you because I'm going to share indie authoring at the 20Books Spain™ and 20Books Holland™ events this week. If I didn't need to be here, I wouldn't be doing this to myself. Mind you, I know I'll be happy I "did" it, just going through jet lag (or considering that I'm about to go through jet lag) has me grumpy as hell.

P.S.S.

MORE STORIES with Michael newsletter HERE: https://michael.beehiiv.com/

ALSO BY THEOPHILUS MONROE

<u>Gates of Eden Universe</u>

<u>The Druid Legacy</u>

Druid's Dance

Bard's Tale

Ovate's Call

Rise of the Morrigan

<u>The Fomorian Wyrmriders</u>

Wyrmrider Ascending

Wyrmrider Vengeance

Wyrmrider Justice

Wyrmrider Academy (Exclusive to Omnibus Edition)

<u>The Voodoo Legacy</u>

Voodoo Academy

Grim Tidings

Death Rites

Watery Graves

Voodoo Queen

<u>The Legacy of a Vampire Witch</u>

Bloody Hell

Bloody Mad

Bloody Wicked

Bloody Devils

Bloody Gods

<u>The Legend of Nyx</u>

Scared Shiftless

Bat Shift Crazy

No Shift, Sherlock

Shift for Brains

Shift Happens

Shift on a Shingle

The Vilokan Asylum of the Magically and Mentally Deranged

The Curse of Cain

The Mark of Cain

Cain and the Cauldron

Cain's Cobras

Crazy Cain

The Wrath of Cain

The Blood Witch Saga

Voodoo and Vampires

Witches and Wolves

Devils and Dragons

Ghouls and Grimoires

More to come!

FREE URBAN FANTASY ADVENTURE: DRUIDESS (GET IT HERE!)

GoE OMNIBUS COLLECTIONS [in Chronological Order]:

The Druid Legacy

Wyrmrider (Books 1-4)

The Voodoo Legacy

The Legacy of a Vampire Witch

The Legend of Nyx

The Vilokan Asylum of the Magically and Mentally Deranged

Other Theophilus Monroe Series

<u>Nanoverse</u>

[Also Available in an Omnibus Edition]

<u>The Elven Prophecy</u>

[Also Available in an Omnibus Edition]

<u>Chronicles of Zoey Grimm</u>

<u>The Daywalker Chronicles</u>

<u>Go Ask Your Mother</u>

AS T.R. MAGNUS

<u>Kataklysm</u>

Blightmage

Ember

Radiant

<u>FREE EPIC: DARKWORLD (GET IT HERE!)</u>

BOOKS BY MICHAEL ANDERLE

Sign up for the LMBPN email list to be notified of new releases and special deals!

https://lmbpn.com/email/

For a complete list of books by Michael Anderle, please visit:

www.lmbpn.com/ma-books/

CONNECT WITH THE AUTHORS

Connect with Theophilus Monroe

Website: www.theophilusmonroe.com

Social Media
https://www.facebook.com/pages/category/Author/
Theophilus-Monroe-Urban-Fantasy-Author-101469961530864/

Connect with Michael Anderle

Website: http://lmbpn.com

Email List: https://michael.beehiiv.com/

https://www.facebook.com/LMBPNPublishing

https://twitter.com/MichaelAnderle

https://www.instagram.com/lmbpn_publishing/

https://www.bookbub.com/authors/michael-anderle

www.ingramcontent.com/pod-product-compliance
Lightning Source LLC
Chambersburg PA
CBHW020154310726
48970CB00006B/2150